LEARNING TO GIVE

LEARNING TO GIVE

HAWTHORN ACADEMY BOOK FOUR

D.R. PERRY

DISRUPTIVE IMAGINATION

THE LEARNING TO GIVE TEAM

Thanks to our Beta Readers

Rachel Beckford and Mary Morris

Thanks to our JIT Readers

Veronica Stephan-Miller, Rachel Beckford, and Kerry Mortimer

Editor
SkyHunter Editing Team

LMBPN Publishing
PMB 196, 2540 South Maryland Pkwy
Las Vegas, NV 89109

Version 1.00, July 2021
(Previously published as a part of the megabook *Hawthorn Academy: Year Two*)
ebook ISBN: 978-1-64971-905-8
Print ISBN: 978-1-64971-906-5

CHAPTER ONE

"I'm heading out!" I hollered up the stairs to my parents, who were still in bed on this lazy Sunday afternoon.

"Drop by Bubbe's first. She's got a gift for you," Mom called back.

"Okay!"

Since I was already almost out the front door, that meant I'd have to go down, out, and back in again through the front entrance to my grandmother's extraveterinary office. It was no big deal; I'd done that a million times over the years.

In the waiting room, I had to stop until Bubbe let me in. It only took a few seconds, but it felt longer than that. I had places to go and friends to see because it was June fifteenth, my seventeenth birthday. Probably, that was why Bubbe wanted to see me too.

Or it could be bad news—about a number of unpleasant things.

"Shush, you."

Yes, I was talking to myself, to a piece of my mind I called the Evil Inside Voice. It had shown up last fall and hadn't gone away since. Personality-wise, it was totally a pessimist and super annoying.

"Aliyah?" Bubbe opened the door behind the counter.

"Hi." I waved. "Mom said you wanted to see me?"

"Yes. I have something for you for your birthday."

My grandmother looked down instead of at me, not her typical behavior. Holidays and special occasions almost always brought her joy. Bubbe usually loved any reason to celebrate, but this day was different, and I should have known why.

"Are you okay?" It might have been my birthday, but I loved my grandma. She's always been there for me and was an amazing person, so I didn't want her suffering.

"A little maudlin is all." Finally, she looked up, the corners of her mouth tilting slightly in a faint grin that didn't touch her eyes. "Come along now."

She held the door open, so I walked through, then stepped aside to let her lead me down the hallway that made up her workspace. Examination rooms lined the hall, each sectioned off by a bisected dutch door. But she didn't bring me into any of those, heading instead into the kitchen.

The space was clean and well-kept as usual, except for the table in the middle. Boxes from the basement covered its surface, ones I recognized from the storage areas down there. Until now, these had been strictly off-limits. Somehow all their surfaces were clean instead of covered by debris, despite long years languishing down in the dustbunny farm.

Either Bubbe had kept it tidy in the storage space, or she'd used some magipsychic device or enchantment to prevent dust from collecting on these. If that was it, the boxes and their contents had to be important to her.

"I promised to tell you all about my brother, the first Noah Morgenstern. We ought to sit down."

I sat, thinking she'd join me, but instead of taking the seat on the other side of the table, my grandmother fiddled with a pair of tall glasses on the counter. She'd prepared iced tea, the kind she often made in summer from the fresh mint in Dad's herb garden.

Patience wasn't my strong suit, but I could manage it for a short and select list of people. Bubbe was first on that list. I sat gazing down at the cover of one scrapbook on the table. It had neon streaks against a deep purple background, reminding me for all the world of the trapper keeper Professor Luciano used in the magipsychic lab at Hawthorn Academy.

I reached out, thinking surely my grandmother wouldn't mind if I had a peek at the photos before her explanation. Her nod as I ran my fingers over the plastic cover confirmed my hunch, so I went ahead and had a look inside.

I recognized my great-grandfather immediately from the many photos on the wall in our apartment upstairs. Unlike the ones in that collection, he stood beside two children instead of just one. Grandma's brother Noah was considerably older than her, unlike the small age difference between my sibling and me.

The first Noah had almost nothing in common with my Noah— physically anyway. The two were practically opposites in that regard. Great Uncle Noah was broad-shouldered instead of beanpole-thin, his smile full and genuine instead of half and ironic, and he was fair-haired instead of dark. He reminded me of someone, in fact.

Me.

You resemble your uncle Richard more.

I rolled my eyes, then noticed that my grandmother had her back to me, thank goodness. I'd let my family in on nearly every secret I'd kept last year at Hawthorn Academy, but not the Evil Inside Voice because I still hoped it'd disappear once I'd spent more time living authentically. Also, I suspected my inner turmoil had more to do with it than any magic.

"Sugar in your tea, Aliyah?" She held the teaspoon over one glass.

"No, thanks. I'll take honey, though, if you have it."

"Of course." Bubbe switched the spoon for the dipper from the honey jar.

A few moments later, after clinking long stirrers around the two tall glasses, Bubbe brought them to the table and sat, pushing the one with honey across to me. I wrapped my hand around it, letting my palm cool against the sweating glass. Even though Bubbe's office had air conditioning, she didn't crank it up until July. She always said it helped the animals in her care know the seasons had changed.

"I hadn't imagined he was so much older than you." With my dry hand, I reached out, tapping the photograph. "Your Noah."

"He might look much older, but he wasn't really." Bubbe pointed at another picture, one where I immediately spotted the difference. "Only four years."

"Oh. So he was big for his age?"

"An early bloomer is what our parents said." Bubbe reached for the page. "I think you'll see something else of interest here."

She'd flipped it over carefully so as not to disturb the pictures pasted in it. They all had that matte look, almost pebbled in true vintage fashion. Glossy wasn't the preferred finish in those days.

I noticed the photo she wanted me to see right away. Great Uncle Noah sat on the beach, just above where the ocean wet the sand. It was dawn, and the person taking the picture did nothing to shield the sun. I saw little besides a silhouette, but one part of it struck me.

"He had a dragonet. Like me." I blinked.

"Yes. A huge surprise to our parents. They thought for sure he'd bond with a tannin, but one day he was out taking a walk, and, well," she said and shook her head, grinning mildly. "It was quite similar to how it happened for you, actually."

"Was he a fire magus? To start with, I mean."

"Solar, like the rest of us Morgensterns. The fire came in later, during his Coast Guard training, so he discovered he was an extram-agus later than you did."

"He was in the service?" I sipped my tea.

"Yes. He introduced me to your grandfather. Brought him home for shore leave right after I graduated from Hawthorn. He ended up winning our wager because of that, too."

"Wager?"

"I said I'd never marry. He bet me two dollars I would fall in love eventually." She smiled softly. "I bet him two more that I'd stay a Morgenstern for the rest of my life. We ended up breaking even."

"Because Grandpa insisted." I returned her smile, remembering stories from my childhood about him saying there were plenty of folks named Smith but almost no magi named Morgenstern.

"That's right."

"Even back then, before the Reveal, your parents were okay with your brother bringing a mundane friend around?"

"He knew about extrahumans. One boat squadron at the Coast Guard was in the know. Back then, with the rise of technology, things had almost gotten untenable. Most of the Salem community figured keeping extrahumans secret wouldn't be possible for much longer."

"I know we'll cover it this year in extrahuman history—the twentieth-century stuff, with the Reveal and everything. Noah said I'd have to do a report on what someone in my family did. Can I use these and make my report about your brother?"

"Yes." She nodded her head once, then held it still. Was this too painful for her? I wanted to take the request back, but she continued, "I'll put them in the spare supply closet so you can get them as needed, but bear in mind, your brother will be jealous."

I sighed. "Why?"

"He didn't have access to any of this last year." Bubbe stared at her hands, laced around the glass of tea. "And that was my mistake. He should have. He's the namesake, after all."

"So, who did he write about?"

"Perhaps you ought to ask him."

"But Bubbe, you know he's not—"

"I know, and you're aware of how I feel about that. The two of you should make up, and this time it's more on him than you."

"I don't understand." I twirled the stirrer in the glass. "Last time you said we both made mistakes. And now, after I got punished for lying, you're saying our issues are his fault?"

"Aliyah, your brother has to learn forgiveness sometime." She shook her head. "Grudges break the person who holds them forever."

"I don't think that'll happen." I shook my head. "Not for a while yet."

"It'll take time, but keep trying." She gazed out the window behind me.

"Do you want to stop talking about your Noah, then? For now, I mean."

"I think I can manage for a while longer. Was there something specific you wanted to know, Aliyah?"

"My brother and yours don't seem much alike. Were you surprised? That I turned out more like him than Noah did?"

"He came late to his abilities, which saved him a good deal of turmoil when he was your age. I wasn't expecting any similarity between the two Noahs, but they are alike in one way. The first Noah Morgenstern had a long and passionate correspondence with a fellow from overseas he met at Hawthorn Academy during an exchange program."

"He was gay?"

"You can read them if you'd like, but yes, they're love letters." My grandmother took a shoebox off the table and opened it briefly to reveal a row of envelopes, then replaced the lid and handed it to me. "Share them with your brother if he asks. He's proud of who he is, but…"

I nodded, studying my grandmother's face. Her eyes were shinier than usual, though not bright. Instead, they reminded me of deep water under moonlight. I imagined the extra reflection in them was hiding grief not given voice for far too long.

"I'll have a look at them eventually." I glanced at the clock on the wall behind her. "My friends are waiting, Bubbe. Sorry, but I gotta go."

"One thing before you leave." My grandmother picked up the smallest box and plucked something from it before closing it again. The item fit so completely in her hand I couldn't see what it was at first. Then she opened her hand, letting part of it drop.

The object dangled, gleaming gold, red, and orange with a hint of blue at the center. She ran the chain through her hand, pulling up the slack until the pendant rested on her palm, then showed it to me. I read the Hebrew inscription twined between the gemstone accents.

"*Shema Yisrael*. Was this his bar mitzvah pendant?" I glanced up at her.

"Yes, it was. And I'd like you to have it," she said, her voice hushed as if she spoke at a graveside.

"Bubbe I couldn't possibly take that from you. It should be Noah's since he's the namesake."

"It's a gift, one I've wanted to pass on for years now. I hope as you explore your great-uncle's past through these letters and photographs, you will understand why it belongs with you and not your brother."

All at once, it made sense. This was a matter of the heart, important to Bubbe, and by extension, important to me because I loved her. If I could honor her this way, I would. I was the one who'd insisted on learning about Great-Uncle Noah. Instead of nodding and turning to leave, I reached out and ran a finger over the pendant.

"It's beautiful." I lifted my gaze, looking my grandmother in the eye. "Thank you. I'll wear it today."

She nodded, swallowing. She'd been on the verge of tears. It reminded me of last year when I tried empathizing with my roommate Grace, who'd lost her parents, imagining how I'd feel if Noah had died. All this time, my grandmother had carried a similar burden, secret from her grandchildren—heavy stuff to ponder on a birthday.

I turned and let her clasp the pendant around my neck. It hung just below the top of my shirt. Before turning around again, I pulled it out from under the fabric.

We hugged briefly but tightly. The moment brightened.

"Thank you, Bubbe." I pulled back enough to look her in the eye. "I love you."

"Happy birthday, Aliyah. I love you, too."

The whisper of shuffling papers and closing albums followed me out of the kitchen and down the hall toward the veterinary office's exit. Soon I'd be out in the bright light of day, in the company of friends and celebrating. I'd appreciate it all the more after the somber start to my day.

CHAPTER TWO

"You're not going to tell us to beware the Ides of June this year, Aliyah?" Izzy raised an eyebrow, then rolled the Skee ball up the lane to score five hundred points. "It's practically a Salem Willows tradition."

"No. After last year, my birthday's nothing to worry about." I chuckled.

"There was a problem last year?" Grace blinked. " I wasn't around, but it couldn't have been that bad, right?"

"Aside from a certain dragonet getting tangled in her hair and Aliyah fleeing the premises after flipping the bird at Noah, everything was great." Dylan smiled, eyes twinkling.

"You didn't tell me she got stuck in your hair." Grace shook her head, reaching down to pat her moon hare's back. "That's a bond right there. Lune practically burrowed into mine the night we met, but nobody saw. Where *is* Ember, anyway?"

"Sleeping in. Bubbe says it's because she's having a growth spurt. And the day we met was pretty embarrassing." I rolled my eyes. "Thanks for sharing, Dylan, even if you left out the part where you almost had to kick me out of here."

"Hey, it's practically my job," he stated. "Someone's got to fill in for

Noah. And Gale's slothful, too. Catching zees like they're endangered or something."

"Making sure we've got plenty of tokens isn't your job anymore, so I guess you've got to do something while you're here." I shrugged.

"How's the job at Walgreens?" Cadence changed the subject. She'd been doing that an awful lot since the end of the school year.

"Boring, but less trouble and way more air-conditioning than I ever had working here." Dylan grinned. "At least campus is climate-controlled."

"You'll appreciate that by the end of July." Cadence nodded at Grace. "It's nice out now, but later on, it can be downright brutal. Figured I'd warn you since you haven't experienced Salem summers. I imagine it gets hotter here than Québec."

"Oh, yeah. I checked the almanacs." Grace fanned herself with a flier advertising open mic night on Sundays at the Witch's Brew. "I could have gone back and worked for my aunt, but my bank account said I couldn't turn down Mr. Ambersmith's job offer. And I get to explore more of the town."

The corners of Dylan's mouth turned down briefly, but the moment he caught me looking, he wiped that look right off his face. I raised an eyebrow, but he turned.

What's he hiding?

"When do you start?" Izzy aimed another Skee ball and threw, missing the five hundred score but managing a hundred and fifty points this time.

"Monday." Grace shrugged with one shoulder. "I'll work eight hour days, but I don't care. It's something I love."

"I think it's awesome, creating works of art people can wear." Cadence clapped her hands. "Will you design your own stuff too? Your costume at Halloween was incredible, and Aliyah tells me your Valentine's dance dress rocked harder than Night Creatures."

"Maybe. I can sketch, draft, and craft whatever patterns I want after hours. They'll even let me use their equipment if I bring my own materials."

"Hey. Why isn't anyone else playing?" Izzy turned, putting her hands on her hips. I noticed she was all out of Skee balls. "I'd like some competition. Why isn't Noah here? He was always good for a couple of rounds."

"He's still not talking to me. And I can't blame him." I sighed and shook my head. "My brother can't abide lying."

"Seriously." Cadence glanced at the open doors. "He's always been a stickler about that. Used to get in the middle of our games in grade school. He'd go nuts if we bent a rule."

"I'll give it a shot." Grace cracked her knuckles. "It can't be harder than Bishop's Row."

As Grace and Izzy set up their Skee Ball games, I turned toward the door to get a breath of fresh air. The light caught my *Shema Yisrael* pendant, flashing a multitude of colors from the gemstones practically in Cadence's face. She squealed, her typical reaction to shiny things.

"Omigod, Aliyah! I can't believe it! Why didn't you show me this? It's gorgeous!"

"Guess I forgot." I winced. "Sorry."

Dylan gave me a look that could have wilted daisies. I'd known Cadence my entire life and she could barely read me, but Dylan, who I'd only known for a year, picked up on my nonverbal cues as adeptly as Izzy. He knew there was no way I'd have forgotten what could only have been a birthday gift.

"It's awesome!" Cadence smiled. "Was it a birthday present? Did it come from your parents?"

"Bubbe, actually. It's a hand-me-down, sort of."

"Wow. Can I take a closer look?"

"Sure, knock yourself out." I leaned against a support beam in the arcade, moving my hair aside so Cadence could examine my pendant.

"It's a hand-me-down, you said? Because it matches your fire magic, like, totally. I can't imagine Bubbe owning something that wasn't all solar."

"Her brother did fire magic, but he passed during the Reveal."

Are you sure nobody suspected he was an extramagus? He was thirteen at his Bar Mitzvah. How could he have had this?

I cleared my throat, which my friends misinterpreted.

"Oh. I didn't know, sorry." Cadence took a step back.

"It's okay. I didn't know about him either until just before school ended." My face felt warmer than the day's temperatures merited.

"What was his name?" Dylan tilted his head.

"Noah." I sighed. "Dad named my brother after him."

"Wow." Cadence shook her head. "I always wonder about my extended family, but my parents never talk about them."

"Are they all, you know, under the sea?" Dylan looked at his shoes, probably trying to think of some less awkward way to phrase the question. Or maybe he couldn't help but make the too-obvious jest and didn't want to come across as mean-spirited.

"I guess." Cadence shrugged. "Anyway, are you ever going to go back to the UK? London, right?"

My eyes widened as I realized Cadence was pulling a Grace. That meant she wasn't cool answering questions about herself, a fairly recent development for my mer-friend. I'd realized last year the best way to avoid giving details about yourself was asking for other people's, and here Cadence was, doing it.

Perhaps she'd learned it working on the school paper at Gallows Hill, or maybe she was hiding something. I'd met her parents, and they were pretty normal for extrahumans. If I didn't know they could grow fins and gills in the ocean, I'd have thought they were shifters or Fae.

"I'm not sure." Dylan shrugged. "Flights are expensive. I can't afford tickets and tuition, even if I work three jobs all summer. Anyway, how's Gallows Hill? Will you ever bring friends from there around?"

"Oh, most of them are nocturnal and don't like being out at this time of day." Cadence looked at just about everything in the arcade except Dylan's face. "Anyway, you'll meet them eventually. Or ask Brianna. You two work together."

Cadence's smile was as brittle as a sea glass orb. Neither friend was comfortable with the other's questions. Pushing them to hash it out in public would have been a jerk move, so I didn't. Eventually, they'd discuss whatever was eating them.

"Anyway, let's go see who's winning Skee Ball." The laugh I attempted sounded more like a nervous titter. "My money's on Grace."

"Oh no, you didn't." Cadence narrowed her eyes, snorting. "You'll catch it if Izzy heard that."

"I'd rather piss off Izzy than Grace, honestly." Dylan winced.

"Come on, guys." I beckoned them toward the Skee Ball lanes, where we spent the rest of the morning watching our friends compete.

After getting home from the Willows, I felt exhausted. Grace and Izzy had gone overboard, competing so intensely that I walked slightly apart from the group on the way home. It was easy to make excuses and leave because my parents and I had dinner plans, just not as early as I let my friends believe.

I couldn't force my friends to get along, but that hadn't been a problem last year. What had changed? I wracked my brain, trying to think of an answer. That was why when I opened the door at the top of the stairs, I almost hit Noah in the face with it.

"Sorry!" I stepped back, blinking.

"Whatever." Noah sailed past me, his elbow colliding with my shoulder. It had to be intentional since he was the same height as me.

"No, I mean it. I'm sorry. About everything." My voice cracked. "Wait, Noah."

Noah said nothing. His footsteps echoed in the stairwell, hollow like the pit of my stomach. All he did last year was run away from me, but somehow, this was worse. We were in our own home, not a campus half-full of bullies hell-bent on dividing us. Now instead of running, he just power-walked like I wasn't important to him anymore.

It was all I could do to keep from sobbing as I shut the door behind me and locked it. Even the familiar weight of Ember landing on my shoulder to greet me didn't offer much comfort.

"Peep?" My dragonet craned her neck until she could look me in the eye.

"I don't know, girl." I sighed and shook my head. "Sorry I didn't bring you out, but you were fast asleep, and I didn't want to wake you."

Ember didn't peep at this, only rubbed her cheek against mine. During the school year, she was always up before me, but lately, my familiar had been sleeping in. I thought it'd be no big deal.

I missed having my little friend around, and apparently, Dylan did too. I stopped in the kitchen, for once not because I was hungry. Out with my friends, it felt too people-y, but being home alone wasn't much better.

"Dad?" I raised my voice, calling through the house. "Mom?"

The door to Mom's home office opened just as I walked past it. That startled me, so I jumped backward, bumping into the counter and knocking over a stool. And here I'd thought I'd outgrown the clumsiness that had plagued me last summer.

"Aliyah. I'm glad you're here. Something came up that I wanted to mention to you." Mom stepped out into the kitchen, closing the door behind her. This was usual because sometimes the stuff she looked at on her computer was confidential.

Mom worked in the Magical Academics Department for the entire state of Massachusetts. She helped with standards and common practice in extrahuman education for both public and private schools, but she also coordinated transfers and special education accommodations for extrahuman students.

"Oh, really?" I blinked. "Me?"

"It seems you'll have a transfer student in your year at Hawthorn come September."

"I guess we have room for one, all things considered." I shrugged, glancing away. The last thing I wanted to do was have another in-depth chat about my dating life.

"Yes. The one fellow who got held back." Mom refrained from uttering his name out loud. That was nice of her, but I'm a big girl and should be able to handle hearing the name of my toxic ex-boyfriend.

"You mean Alex Onassis." I raised an eyebrow, refusing to give him the Lord Voldemort treatment in my own home.

"Yes, the one who scored so spectacularly low on his final exam, who went from a B minus to failing in sixty minutes."

"And people wonder where I get my capacity for sass from." I smiled.

"Well, you know what they say about fire magi." My mother chuckled.

"Our burns are sick?"

We ended up in a knock-down drag-out laugh-fest. Minutes later, we leaned on the counter, gasping for air and holding our sides. It felt like both of us needed a good laugh, or really, all three of us. Ember was in the same state on the countertop, curled around the fruit basket for support.

I opened the fridge, produced a pitcher of lemonade, and poured us two glasses. I even splashed some into a small bowl for Ember, who lapped it up, then smacked her lips and stuck her tongue out like a toddler eating a Sour Patch kid. After that, I gave her water in another dish and we drank together, eventually recovering from the laugh-in.

"So, tell me about this new student." I poured more lemonade. "Why the transfer?"

"He bonded with a familiar during his last week at his old school. Unexpectedly, but that happens sometimes. His family reached out and asked if it was possible for him to attend Hawthorn."

"Oh?" I tried to hide the intensity of my curiosity. I had a million questions about the mysterious new student but wouldn't be able to ask them all. "Why did they call you?"

"I went to middle school with his mother."

"So he's from Providence?" I blinked. "Was he at Trout?" Trout Academy was a prep school for magi and changelings down in Rhode Island.

"No." Mom took a deep breath. "The Academy."

"The what now?" I almost dropped my glass, lemonade and all. The Academy was practically juvie, despite its pricey tuition and fancy branding as a place for young extrahumans to learn self-discipline.

"You heard me. Since you're both on disciplinary probation next year, I'm sure you'll run into him more than you might expect. There are study requirements you'll have in common."

"I thought Familiar Bonding was just for first-years."

"He'll need that since he's new to familiars. Second-years on probation have a mandatory study hall, one they spend with the previous year's top student as a mentor."

"Oh? The top student?" I shake my head. "Hal's in the infirmary half the time, so he's got no time to mentor anyone."

"The top student last year wasn't Hal Hawkins. It was Logan Pierce."

"What?" I blinked. "Wow. I'm proud of him, but I had no idea."

"That's the other reason I wanted to talk to you. I was just about to call the Pierces, speak with Logan, and inform him about the extra responsibility next year. But from what you and Bubbe have told me, his home life is complex."

"You could say that." I wasn't sure how much off-record information Mom had about Logan's dysfunctional family. Between my friendship with him and Noah's with his older sister Elanor, Bubbe knew just about everything.

"Maybe you could join the call with me. It might help for Logan to see a familiar face. We're dropping an unexpected change on him, after all."

"I think you're right, Mom," I said, nodding. She knew about Logan's accommodations at school. He wasn't a typical learner and had unconventional strategies to deal with it. "Sure. It'll be nice to see him, even if it's only on a screen."

Logan Pierce had been one of my best friends at school last year. We got so close, people made bets on when we'd date. We decided to stay platonic like I am with Izzy or Cadence, a relief for both of us.

Mom went into her office. I let her have privacy for the information she handled. It wasn't easy, especially not after what she did last summer.

Mom had secretly gone down to Providence, testifying on official record against her own brother without telling any of us, not even Dad. We didn't find out until Passover, when she brought the news clipping as her symbol of liberation. She'd freed herself from the toxic half of her family finally and totally with that act.

Could she be hiding something personal in her office among work stuff that everyone steered clear of for legal reasons? Yes. Would she? Again, yes. It wasn't easy to deal with the idea that your mother had survived childhood by using judicious dishonesty, especially not while I was still trying to figure out who I wanted to be.

I was lucky at the same time because each person in my immediate family gave me different examples. Some of my other friends had it worse, and sharing our problems gave us all more perspective.

Mom opened the door again, letting me into her office. She had her video conferencing computer pointed at the bookcase behind her, which was mostly for show. She did sometimes use a few of those books but kept it tidy. This would be an asset when calling the Pierces.

Logan's parents were all about how things looked, though not in a professional or stodgy sort of way. They were a showbiz family, so fixated and focused on being flashy that all of Logan's academic and other achievements didn't matter to them. They disparaged his artwork and his grades, saying they'd never look good on stage.

Mom pulled up a chair for me to sit beside her in the camera's range. We waited through the chimes as the conference call software made its connection. It was early in the morning in Las Vegas, which was where Logan's family lived, but the call was part of a calendar agenda displayed on Mom's screen, with invitations given and accepted. Apparently, they'd agreed to it.

When someone answered, the camera turned on so we could see the other end of the call. I hadn't formally met Logan's parents, just seen them in passing at Parents' Night last fall. They'd largely ignored Logan, lavishing most of their attention on his sister Elanor. But today, the entire family hadn't shown up. Only one of them answered the call.

"Good morning Mrs. Pierce." Mom's tone was cool and professional, designed to keep things calm.

"What's this about then?" Mrs. Pierce stretched, stifling a yawn.

"You can't possibly want to talk to Logan." She gave me a side-eye Izzy would have envied.

"As a matter of fact, I do." My mother gave a slight nod. "Headmaster Hawkins asked me to inform him about a special assignment starting this fall."

"Then why isn't the headmaster calling?" She closed her eyes. "Unless this isn't an assignment. He screwed up again. I knew he couldn't handle things at Hawthorn, not with his disability."

I sat blinking, my mouth wide open. Logan told me about how his parents made him feel lesser and not good enough. I thought it was only about performance art, which Logan only did under duress. But there she was, dragging his name through the dirt, and he wasn't even there to defend himself.

Mom's face stayed neutral, almost stony. Clearly, she'd heard this sort of thing before from parents. The fact that it was all too common from her perspective turned my stomach.

"Mrs. Pierce, your son had the highest grade point average in his year. That's why he's being asked to mentor a transfer student this fall."

"That's impossible." She clicked her tongue against the top of her mouth. "Not that he couldn't make grades with enough outside help." She glanced at me. "But he's been to your house, so you know what I'm saying. Logan can't do this. He's not normal. Can't even look people in the eye when they talk to him. My son's no mentor."

"He helped plenty of us last year, you know." I couldn't keep my mouth shut any longer. "Logan's got some of the best study tips we've ever heard. I even use them."

"Yes. Aliyah, right?" She raised an eyebrow. "I hear *you're* on probation."

"Not academically." I grinned. "In large part, thanks to my good friend Logan."

"Is that Aliyah?" Logan's voice was muffled, coming from the other side of a closed door behind Mrs. Pierce. "Can I talk to her?"

"Part of the purpose of this call is to discuss this with Logan. I'd appreciate his presence." My mother nodded.

"I'm not sure I'll permit him to do this."

"Mrs. Pierce, your son will be seventeen this summer."

"Well, yes, but that doesn't mean he's an adult."

"In the Massachusetts Magical Academics Department, it does. He can make certain decisions about his schooling the year before he's a legal adult. Your permission is not required."

"Well, I never." She shook her head. "He's still sixteen for another two months, and this is Nevada. Nothing here says I have to let him talk to you."

"That's true." My mother nodded. "I'll simply send him a certified letter instead. You can expect that next week. Or you can allow us to have this chat, and you won't be bothered in the future."

"I think you ought to send the letter, Mrs. Morgenstern." She stifled a yawn again, but this time it looked different, as though she'd faked one of them. I couldn't figure out which. "The difference between our time zones is inconvenient. My son shouldn't make decisions without a proper night's sleep. He had a very late night, rehearsing for our new show. I'm sure you understand."

"Perfectly." My mother's smile could have cut diamonds. "I'll send the letter then. Remember, it requires his matching signature, which I have on file."

"I know what certified mail is." She waved as if she sat on a parade float instead of a tufted chair. "Good day."

The screen went blank. I didn't even get a chance to talk to my friend. It occurred to me I could have begged a few moments on account of my birthday, but it was too late for that. I needed to think more quickly in the future.

"Mom, are the other parents always like this?" I shook my head. "How do you deal with it?"

"I have a unique blend of perspective and experience when it comes to these issues." She shut down the software. "It's unfortunate, but we always do what's best for the student. At least the laws in our state allow for that."

"Is this why you chose Hawthorn? For the academic program?"

"To help people like me, yes." She looked up at me, eyes rimmed with the red of unshed tears—the angry kind. "I got my wish. To be the person I needed at that age."

"They're lucky to have you, Mom." I stood up. I would have offered her a hug, but sometimes when Mom got like this, she needed the distraction of work. "Can I get you anything? More lemonade?"

"No, I've got to print that letter and get it to the post office as soon as possible." Mom made a few clicks with her mouse, doing exactly that. "But when I get back, how about we go get a coffee? Something fancy over at the Witch's Brew. It's your birthday, after all."

"Sounds great, Mom."

I got out of her way, and less than twenty minutes later, we sat in the coffee house, having a nice afternoon together. I wished Logan the same, no matter how unlikely he was to get it in the near future.

CHAPTER THREE

It was hotter inside than outside, typical for August. The house at 10 1/2 Hawthorne Street didn't have central air, a fact my father lamented in the kitchen that morning. Bubbe's office did, but we didn't have a compressor for the top two floors. There was nothing we could do about it in the immediate future, either. Not unless one of us befriended an ice magus.

"I'm going out!" I hollered to my parents as I grabbed my knapsack off the floor near the front door.

"Where?" Mom's voice from the office.

"Dunno, someplace cool." I had the front door open but didn't want to leave until getting the go-ahead.

"Have fun!"

With that permission, I headed out the door and down the front stairs, not bothering to lock up behind me as I jogged down the driveway. At the end, I stopped, already wiping sweat off my brow.

"Peep?" Ember circled my head, waiting for me to pick up the pace.

"It's hot out here for me." I chuckled. "Must be perfect for you, though."

My dragonet's element was fire. She breathed it, so a day with high temperatures wouldn't bug her. She didn't land on my shoulder, probably because it was too slippery from the humidity and the insta-sweat that went along with it on dog days like this. I'd taken a shower ten minutes earlier, too.

"Peep!" Ember pointed her nose directly at Izzy's house, which was in front of mine.

"Yeah, that was the plan." I turned the corner and headed up to the door, ringing the bell at the apartment, not the divination parlor. Isabella Mendez, my best friend, was also from a family that lived and worked in the same building, except their spaces were side by side instead of stacked, and her family were clairvoyant psychics instead of magi.

The door opened, revealing my friend. She was shorter than me, like most girls I know, and practically everything about her appearance was opposite. Her hair and skin were dark while mine were fair, and she favored buns and braids on the sides of her head instead of up top or in back. We both wore messy buns that day because nobody needed hair sticking to sweaty faces.

"Oh, no way." Izzy crossed her arms over her chest and shook her head. "I'm not going to the Willows. The Tanks are down there."

"So what?" I shook the bag of leftover Arcade tokens. The Tanks were the local shifter gang and Izzy was not a fan, a point of contention between her and Cadence. "It's boiling, and we want the beach."

"Can't we go to Hawthorn and swim in the baths?" She sighed. "Messing doesn't have anything like a pool. And besides, they're closed all summer."

" Last time I tried to stop by, the headmaster said I can't come in. Probation sucks." I shrugged. "I can only go on campus if he approves it and I've got an escort."

"Oh. Sorry." Izzy stared at her flip-flop-clad feet. "I still can't believe it's this big a deal after all this time."

"Well, lying about being an extramagus is a pretty colossal mistake to make at my school."

"Magi." Izzy looked back up, shaking her head and clucking her tongue. "So uptight. It's no big deal at Messing if someone's psychic and a vampire or whatever. I can't understand why it's even a thing."

"Because psychics don't end up with a case of mixed nuts from having extra...extrahumanness, I guess." I shrugged. "But we're boiling out here. Literally." I indicated the sweat beading on my forehead.

"Okay, I get it. Let's go."

"But where?"

"How about tracking down our literal breath of fresh air?" Izzy waggled her eyebrows, then stuck her tongue out like we were still seven.

She meant Dylan, of course. If it were Cadence making that face and suggestion, I'd get angry at her for being crass about a guy who's in a relationship. But Izzy was probably just making a dad joke.

"I think he's working, anyway." I shrugged the jest off. "That boy's middle name should be workaholic."

"So, let's go to Walgreens and get a soda or something." Izzy beckoned. "It's air-conditioned."

We headed to the sidewalk, turning toward Derby Street and the drugstore. Besides Dylan, Brianna worked there. She was a goblin changeling who went to Gallows Hill with Cadence.

Salem was one of those towns where you could do everything or nothing almost any day of the year. It was magical, literally and figuratively, but also mundane, especially in summer. Nobody thought much about witches riding on brooms, jack-o'-lanterns, or tumbling particolored leaves during the dog days of August. Not even the signs declaring this the witch city could fight thermometers screaming one hundred degrees Fahrenheit.

The blacktop parking lot and glass veneer of Walgreens focused the heat. I imagined this was how a bug felt under a magnifying glass in the sun, wielded by some sociopathic little tyke. My mind dreamed up a kindergarten-aged version of Alex Onassis.

"Ugh." I shook my head and wrinkled my nose, wishing I hadn't thought of him. Maybe Izzy was right to stay unentangled romantically. Breaking up had side effects, apparently.

"Yeah, I know." Izzy pointed at the door. "If you can't take the heat, get into the Walgreens."

"Peep!"

Ember soared toward the door, dipping and weaving through the air in front of it. There was nothing quite like worrying about my familiar crashing headlong into a plate-glass window to motivate me, so I opened the door and let her fly through, following close behind.

The welcome blast of cold air blew my hair away from my forehead. When walking into a warm building after being outside in frigid temperatures, people exhale. But opposite conditions were opposite, so I breathed in as much of the artificial coolness as possible. Then I tripped over my own feet and landed flat on my face on the doormat.

"Oh, no!" Hurried footsteps chased the exclamation.

The set of hands helping me up was also nice and cold, but they didn't belong to Dylan Khan. My rescuer was Brianna Collins, and it was awfully nice of her. Nobody was obliged to pick a klutz up off the floor, so I appreciated it.

"Thanks, Brianna." My face was red and flushed, but I still hoped everyone in the store thought it was just because of the ungodly heat outside. "Flip-flops conspired against me just then. Sorry."

"Aliyah, seriously?" Brianna shook her head. Was her face a bit ruddy, too? "No need to apologize. I'm sorry."

"Sorry." I brushed off my hands, besmirched by the welcome mat. Or maybe the unwelcome mat, all things considered.

"Jeez, this is getting old, and you've only been doing it all summer." Izzy pulled a bottle of Sprite out of a cooler nearby, then handed it to me. "You just apologized after being told you don't need to apologize. Somebody's Canadian." Izzy's forehead wrinkled as she patted her satchel of tarot cards. "Like, for real. Someone in here."

"Did somebody call for aid from the Great North?" A grinning face peeked out from behind a Hallmark display. "Hi!"

Grace Dubois waved, a card in her hand. She gulped before lowering it, and I saw a pastel floral illustration on the cover. A streak of gray rounding the corner on the floor distracted me. Lune was here too, and clearly happy to see Ember. The dragonet landed, and they hopped around on the floor together.

"So, the Ambersmiths let you go out today?"

"Yeah, it's a supply run." Grace sauntered from behind the shelf, pushing a collapsible shopping cart piled high with snacks. "Everyone down at the shop is hungry, thirsty, and tired, so they sent me out."

"I've barely seen you since my birthday back in June. They must be working you hard. We missed you." The silence that followed that statement was less than comfortable, but I wasn't sure why.

"Yeah, I get it." She chuckled, glancing over her shoulder. Her knuckles whitened around her grip on the cart's handle. "Anyway, I should check out and get going."

"I'll help." Izzy stepped up, grabbing an arm full of assorted sodas from the cooler and walking them up to the counter. An apologetic wince twisted her expression. "Gives us time to chat."

"Thanks. I hadn't gotten the drinks yet." Grace nodded once. "I appreciate it."

"Right. It's almost like I'm a mind reader or something." Izzy chuckled. And just like that, the tension between my friends broke.

Everybody laughed. Izzy had that effect on people, getting them to laugh with her instead of at her. And if there was one thing Grace loved in this world—besides Lune—it was a good laugh.

As Brianna rang up Grace's purchases and they did the whole transaction, we chattered away about the heat. I couldn't believe we only talked about the stupid weather. Something still felt wrong, like my friends were avoiding some subject. I figured it couldn't hurt to mention someone we all had in common.

"So, how's Dylan?"

Everybody shut up. I just stood there blinking like an idiot, because I would never have guessed he was the forbidden topic.

Your circus, your monkeys.

"Was he fired or something?" Could Dylan Khan, the hardest-working teenager I knew next to Grace, have lost his job? It was the only reason I could think of for all the awkwardness.

"No, nothing like that." Brianna let out a nervous laugh. "Maybe he's working at Hawthorn."

"I was wondering about campus, actually." I picked up a pack of gum and twirled it in my hands, trying to find something to help me feel less awkward. "Izzy mentioned having a swim in the baths to cool off, but I can't go because of probation. Do you think the headmaster would give me permission? And would you be our escort?"

Brianna blinked because she knew almost nothing about Hawthorn's policies, but Grace shook her head.

"I've no idea. I haven't been to campus all summer."

"Oh. Okay." I tried to keep my expression neutral. Grace had a bad habit of bottling things up, to the point where last year she'd had a mental health crisis. Her counselor was Headmaster Hawkins, so I worried but didn't say anything about it in front of the others.

"I'm still having meetings about school stuff." Grace elbowed my arm. "But at the shop after hours, not on campus. Sorry, I can't help you."

"Well, what about Lee being your escort? He'd do it for Izzy."

I nearly jumped out of my skin because I didn't expect to hear a voice right behind me. But at least it was familiar, so I settled down quickly.

"For crying out loud, Cadence." Izzy snorted. "I don't want to date anyone."

"I'm not saying you do. But he's on campus." Cadence shrugged, her red-orange hair cascading over one shoulder. "Sorry about listening in, but I love swimming, and Lee's cool. We haven't been out since Aliyah's birthday."

"I guess you have a point." Izzy sighed so much she practically deflated. "Sorry I haven't been around."

"Me too." Grace shrugged.

"Yeah, sorry." I grinned, predicting the response.

"Aliyah, stop apologizing!" Izzy stomped her foot. Something had her more on edge than a spinning coin.

There's only one thing to do about that.

"What's your problem today, Iz?" I leaned against the counter.

"Peep?" Ember perched on my head, which probably made me look ridiculous at a serious moment.

"Fine. I'm pissed off. Yeah, I'm being a bitch. Said I was sorry already."

"So talk about it." Grace put a bag of snacks into the cart, sighing. "I mean, you can't ignore all your problems. It's not healthy."

"This isn't the place." Izzy shook her head. "But yeah, I need to talk about next year. Probably we all should. As many of us as possible."

"Even me?" Brianna's eyes widened.

"Yeah, I guess." Izzy flipped a tarot card on the counter between them, then swept it away before I saw anything besides the Cups suit.

"I work until six." She glanced at the register. "If that's too late, I understand."

"It's not. That's good for dinner at Engine House." I pointed diagonally across the street at my favorite pizza place. "Let's meet there later. It's air-conditioned."

"I have to go back to work, but I'll see you later. And I'm bringing Dylan." Grace didn't smile, but she waved and headed out, pushing the cart.

CHAPTER FOUR

Cadence, Izzy, and I headed down Derby Street, making our way toward Winter Island Park. We loved the Willows, but Winter Island had the best swimming area within walking distance.

Tourists blanketed the sand, towel-covered spaces headed up with umbrellas and beach chairs. That never bothered us. As locals, we weren't shy about using our town's resources. Ember got excited as soon as she saw the ocean. She loved swimming.

We dropped our towels and the clothes we wore over our swim-suits, then headed for the water to jump right in. It was cold, briny, and exactly what we needed on a day where the temperature flirted with one hundred degrees even without the heat index. Cadence swam circles around us because she's a mermaid, which meant she'd turned her legs into a finned and scaled tail.

She splashed water in my face and I laughed. From behind us, I heard a chorus of delighted squeals and gasps. On the beach stood a gaggle of kids about middle-school age. The redhead pointed and the jet-haired girl beside her jumped up and down. The olive-complected boy with them tilted his head, blinking for all the world like a cat who'd just woken up from a nap. The fourth, a pallid younger boy, dropped the book he held. He shrugged at something the other boy said, then retrieved the tome, shaking sand off its pages.

I got the impression the kids were extrahumans. Probably shifters, though the boy with the book could have been a magus or a psychic. Cadence waved, smiling at them and flipping her tail out of the water. Whenever kids noticed her, she always put on a good show. Before the Reveal, she wouldn't have been allowed to swim in public, so I never got on her case for showing off mermaid-style.

"We're just trying to swim. Why do we have to show off for tourists all the time?" Izzy rolled her eyes. "Do they think this is Tahiti?"

"Come on, Izzy, they're kids. Salem's a magical place." Cadence grinned. "If you'd never seen the tail before, you'd react the same way."

"She definitely did the first time she saw it," I said, splashing at my friends.

"Yeah, okay. You got me there." Izzy rolled over on her back, floating. She gazed up at the brassy blue sky.

The cold water lifted our spirits, and so did Ember. Her swimming antics were hilarious. At times she swam like a duck, wings folded over her back, her peeping reminding me of baby mallards at the end of spring. Sometimes she dived, waving her serpentine tail in the air. At one point she came up with a mouthful of seaweed, spitting and spluttering because that was not part of a fire dragonet's balanced diet.

I laughed so hard I got a cramp and had to leave the water. As a mermaid, Cadence didn't have that problem. Izzy was in a solemn mood, limiting her laughter to chuckles.

I was wringing my hair out at the line the water made with the sand when the two girls who'd been watching Cadence ran up to me.

"Ask her, Hope," the brunette whispered.

"You ask her, Saya." Hope shrugged.

"I can't." Saya blinked.

"Hi, girls." I gave them my friendliest smile. "What can I do for you?"

"I don't know." The brunette's shoulders shook. She mumbled something else.

"My friend just wanted to know if that's really a dragonet," Hope asked, smiling.

"She sure is. Her name's Ember, do you want to meet her?" My familiar loved people, especially kids.

The brunette only nodded. I whistled, and Ember took off from the surface of the water. She landed on the sand between the girls and me and hopped toward them.

"Peep?" She swayed her head up and down, a serpentine nod.

"Wow." Hope held her hand down. She knew something about magical creatures, then. Saya copied her. I got the impression they'd known each other for years.

Ember hopped up and down, capering and carrying on playfully.

"Cool." The catlike boy sauntered over, grinning from ear to ear. "That's not something we see every day in Newport."

"You're sure we won't get in trouble, Cosmo?" Saya glanced over her shoulder.

"Relax. Your bro's cool. Um, not literally." The boy tried to put his hands in his pockets, but his swim trunks didn't have any. He blushed.

"You guys." The smaller boy tilted his head as though listening to someone who wasn't there. It reminded me of Izzy's grandfather, who was a medium. "Bob says we gotta go. Sandwiches are almost gone."

"Fewmets." Cosmo glanced over his shoulder. "Race ya!"

Both the boys ran back up the beach toward an umbrella about halfway up.

"Thanks, Miss." The little brunette gave me an actual curtsy. "Ember's adorable."

"You're welcome." I wasn't sure how to curtsy, so I bowed instead.

"Bye, Ember!" Hope waved, then grabbed Saya's hand and ran after the boys.

"Hey, Aliyah!" someone called. I turned to see who it was. Waving from under an umbrella was my friend from school, Faith Fairbanks.

We hadn't always been friendly. Last fall, we got into plenty of arguments, but we were past that by winter break last year. That was a good thing since we'd leaned on each other pretty heavily last spring. I headed over to say hello.

She sat with her boyfriend, Hal Hawkins. He looked better than the last time I'd seen him, but that was not saying much. He had a debilitating chronic illness with no cure, but at least he felt well enough to be at the beach that day.

"How are you guys? I've barely seen you all summer."

"Not too bad," Hal said, "The doctors down in Boston have helped a bit. I'll probably go into town every other weekend after school starts to keep up with the treatments."

"So, your mom hasn't been giving you any trouble?" I raised an eyebrow. Hal's mother used to be in charge of his health care, but that had changed recently in family court.

"Nothing that affected my treatment." He grinned. "More of a puzzle. But I'm dealing with it."

"You're going too easy on her." Faith patted Seth, the small critter in her lap. He was a sha, a canine species with undeath magic, affiliated with magi since ancient Egypt. "She screamed at us this morning. Nin hasn't come out of my beach tote all afternoon."

The hibiscus-printed bag leaning against the umbrella pole quivered slightly. Ember peeped softly at it. A few little squeaks came from its open top, but Hal's familiar didn't emerge. Nin was a Pharaoh's rat, something like a cross between a mongoose and a ferret with space magic.

"Fair point." Hal gestured at an insulated bag between them. "Would you like an apple?"

Hal looked younger than the rest of us, in part because of his illness, but he acted more like an adult, probably for the same reason. And suddenly, despite the salt air and all the swimming earlier, I wasn't hungry. But the offer of food reminded me of something.

"We're going to Engine House for dinner like around six o'clock. If you guys are still in town, do you want to come?"

"That sounds great." Faith smiled, a rare expression for her even on a good day. "My train back to New York doesn't leave from Boston until ten."

"Sounds great. See you then." I waved, then headed back down the beach and toward Izzy and Cadence, who were still in the water.

I didn't know that dinner would be more awkward than awesome.

I got to Engine House first, so I went straight to the back toward the largest table. This one had a booth along the back wall with tables and then chairs on the other side. We'd need as many seats as possible. Instead of perching, Ember swooped through the air, making figure eights. Other patrons at the restaurant watched the show she put on.

"You must be excited, huh?" I smiled at my dragonet.

"Peep!"

"It's been a while since you've seen Gale, I totally get it." I didn't need to go into detail about how I missed her friend's magus, which was inappropriate. Dylan was with Grace, so only Ember knew about my feelings for him. And my brother Noah, who'd guessed it last year and hadn't mentioned the matter since.

Not that I had any idea what to do about them besides keep my mouth shut. My dating experience included a discussion with Logan where we agreed to stay platonic and a dating-by-default situation with Alex the mega-jerk.

I'd ended things with Alex by asserting myself. Izzy and Cadence had helped me realize what was wrong with that relationship. To say Alex hadn't been happy would be a massive understatement. He'd practically vowed revenge at the end of last year. My friends and I, even the ones from town, had to watch our backs.

They'd be on campus for extramurals between all three of our schools, a simultaneously exciting and scary prospect. Most of my friends from school and town got along, but Izzy and Grace hadn't stopped competing all summer. Cadence had just adopted a blasé attitude toward everything except boys.

Maybe that was the point of this dinner, part of the reason Grace recommended we sit down and talk. Hal and Faith might inject some solidarity into the group. They had been good at that last year. I'd do everything I could to help us avoid trouble once school started. My friends deserved no less.

One good thing about my seat in the back was visibility. I could see all the windows from here, and saw when Brianna approached the restaurant, tucking her Walgreens apron into the satchel over her shoulder. She pushed through the door, ducking slightly. She didn't need to since the door was tall enough, but I understood. She was self-conscious about being tall and lanky.

"Hey, Aliyah!" She scooted into the booth to sit beside me. "I know I'm early, but that's when they let me out, so here I am." Her grin seemed real, but the little laugh sounded nervous.

We'd hung out during breaks from school last year. She was not quite this awkward then, but maybe the impending extramurals had her on edge. School wasn't easy for Brianna. She'd mentioned getting flack about being a goblin changeling before.

"Hey, yourself." I smiled back. "I already ordered a pizza mountain and two pitchers of soda, but if you want something else, you can add it to the tab. My grandma just paid me for helping out in her office."

"No, I'm good, thanks." Brianna folded her hands on the table, looking down at them. "Anyway, before everyone else gets here, I was wondering—"

She didn't complete her sentence because Izzy showed up. She sat directly across from me in the chair by the window. Right away, she looked over her shoulder, jerking her thumb at the door.

"Cadence is here, but she's outside talking to some bruiser." Izzy rolled her eyes.

"Oh, that's Bar." Brianna jerked a thumb at the door, where Cadence chattered animatedly at a tall, wide, and solidly built fellow with a thick steel bar piercing his septum. "I bet you can see why they call him that."

"Yeah, I get it." I wondered where I'd seen that guy before. "He looks familiar."

"He was at the concert on Halloween with Cadence and Crow." She raised her eyebrows at me, then glanced at Izzy. Whatever she was trying to convey nonverbally fell short of my comprehension.

"Right." I nodded. "I remember now. Bar's a troll changeling and Crow's some sort of bird shifter. Cadence said they don't work at the Gallows Hill newspaper with her. "

"Exactly. Crow said he'd help this year. She talked him into it."

"Mermaid, magic voice, duh." Izzy rolled her eyes but smiled.

"What's the holdup?" I asked.

"She's trying to convince him to hang with us." Izzy shrugged. "I don't think it'll happen."

"Why?" I blinked.

"Troll changelings are hardheaded in more ways than one." Izzy rapped her knuckles on the side of her head.

"Yeah, her mermaid stuff doesn't work on them." Brianna smiled.

"Maybe it's a good thing." Izzy gestured at the remaining seats. "We won't have room with everybody else we invited."

"Normally I'd say the more the merrier, but you've got a point, Iz." I nodded.

"Cadence would rather have Crow here than Bar." Brianna repeated her mysterious eyebrow raise.

"What's this all about then?" Izzy narrowed her eyes.

"She's got a crush, but what else is new?" Brianna let out that nervous laugh again.

"Yeah, what else is new?" Izzy shrugged. "Tons, apparently, that she hasn't told me. Or her parents, probably. But enough about Cadence. What are you up to?"

"Just working, mostly." Brianna fiddled with the empty cup in front of her. "Trying not to freak out about playing Bishop's Row at extramurals this year."

"Am I the only one who isn't bothered by any of this?" I blinked. "It'll be fun."

"You told us an influential new first-year is a magisupremacist, and you're not worried?" Izzy raised her eyebrow.

"Well, crap." I winced.

Cadence walked through the door, shaking her head as she strode briskly toward us. She took the seat on the other side of Brianna.

"What now?" Cadence asked.

"I'm a little more worried about next year than I was previously." I grimaced. "Thanks to our psychic friend."

Izzy lifted her hand, giving us all a little golf wave and a parade-float smile.

"Better nervous and prepared than confident without a clue. At least that's what my parents say." Cadence rolled her eyes. " But won't it be fun? A little danger's exciting sometimes."

"Okay." I blinked. "You know how most of us feel about that kind of thing, Cadence. Danger bad."

"Life is danger, friends. You either sink or swim." Cadence's smile had never reminded me of a shark's until that day. "Lucky for you, I'm an expert, and I've been coaching Grace. She's got a plan for this year."

"Yeah, you're a daredevil." Izzy nodded. "The two of us have vetoed all your dangerous ideas since forever. Of course you're going into next year like it's the nineties and we're in the X-games."

I waved at the door, probably more frantically than I had to.

"Look, there's Lee." I had to change the subject or Izzy and Cadence would drag on each other for another ten minutes. Thankfully, my classmate's arrival stopped that before it began.

"Hello." Lee grinned and sat beside Izzy. When she glanced at him, the corners of her mouth turned up, and her previously tense shoulders eased down a notch.

"I've got your Sprite and your Coke here." The pitchers of soda settled themselves on the tabletop because the waiter was a psychic, the telekinetic kind. "Root beer's coming with your pizza in just a few minutes. How many plates do you need?"

"Nine, I think," I answered.

"Better make that ten. I ran into Azrael on the way here." Lee added.

"Great." Izzy leaned back to drag another chair from the table behind us. "Exactly what I needed."

"I don't think he'll bug you much anymore, Iz." Cadence leaned her elbows on the table, folded her hands, and set her chin on them.

"Oh?" Izzy blinked. "What happened?"

"Rumor has it he's moved on." Cadence studied her pearl-pink fingernails.

"Rumor?" Izzy side-eyed the mermaid. "You're not even at school with him. Haven't been for months."

"You think just because I'm not on campus, it means there's no gossip to follow?" Cadence snorted. "I'm good at my job."

The bell over the door jingled as Hal walked in with Faith.

"Guys, we're here, but there's a problem." Faith approached the table, Hal straggling behind her. She jerked her thumb at the window to my right.

We all looked outside to see an unfolding scene that could have come straight out of a teen movie.

CHAPTER FIVE

Dylan and Grace stood outside the window, light from inside spilling shadows long and stark on the sidewalk and into the street next to the Engine House. The window framed them, letting us see more than we probably should have.

Grace had her arms crossed over her chest, her posture as straight and defiant as if she were facing down a monster. And maybe one lurked out there in the street that night, some awful presence between the two—a monster they couldn't agree whether to capture or slay.

Dylan stood with one hand out, shoulders shaking, head down. I knew he dared to look in her eyes because he faced me. He pleaded with her, begging for something she couldn't or wouldn't give.

I'd never seen him like this, not even on the day he and Logan had experienced the strain and drama of bonding with familiars they thought were wrong for them. Dylan Khan had accused me last year of wearing my heart on my sleeve, but he'd always seemed opposite: able to hide his feelings behind a six-foot hedge of quirkiness.

Whatever he said to Grace that night, it left her unmoved. Their discussion was a mystery to us, even after she shook her head and walked past him toward the restaurant's door. He followed her, head down, with one shaky hand reaching up to fling tears from his eyes.

Neither spoke about the scene outside, but Cadence patted the seat beside her, glancing up at Grace. And Hal and Faith moved down so Dylan could sit between them and Lee instead of across from her.

Our pizzas came out then, floating over from behind the counter to settle on the table at evenly spaced intervals. The psychic waiter used his powers to bring us our order, including the root beer. As amusing as this usually was, it didn't cheer me up, because my friends carried the burden of whatever had passed between them on the street.

Dylan's nickname at school was "the bottomless pit." His dragonet, Gale, usually snapped up any scraps he left behind, but that night, Gale stayed tucked around his neck, sleeping. Dylan barely managed one slice of pizza, leaving sauce and cheese along with the crust and a few stray slivers of mushroom on the plate. Grace wolfed down almost half a pie on her own, chasing it with so much root beer we had to order another pitcher.

When Azrael Ambersmith walked in the door, Dylan excused himself, leaving his nearly full paper plate, a half-glass of Sprite, and bewildered friends. Azrael didn't take the vacated seat, instead squeezing into the booth beside Grace. He raised an eyebrow at the crumb-filled plate in front of her, then glanced at me.

"What do I owe you?"

"Nothing." I fidgeted, wishing I could go after Dylan before he got to campus because I couldn't follow him there until school started. "Bubbe technically paid, so thank her next time you see her."

"What was that?" Izzy raised her eyebrow.

"Um, don't you know?" I wanted to keep Grace out of Izzy's hot seat. "Psychic friend?"

"Yeah." She shrugged, then for the first time in over a year, Izzy did emotional triage. "But we're here for a reason. Stuff to hash out before school starts."

"I'll check on him." Hal tried standing but fell back in his seat and rolled his eyes. "I guess not. Stupid body. They just don't make them like they used to in my family."

"Not funny." Faith shook her head. "But I get it. I'll go."

Faith nodded to me as she stood, pushing the chair in behind her. I watched Nin scuttle out of her tote to Hal's shoulders, Seth peeking out to yip goodbye as she left the restaurant.

"Let's do this already." Grace snagged another slice of pizza. "You know, the talking about the tension stuff."

"Okay, Grace." Izzy leaned on the table, hands flat against its wooden surface. "We get stuck in moments, which is a good thing in life-threatening crises. But if we can't move forward, we end up with patterns, like unwanted rivalry." She glanced at me. "And default relationships."

"She's right." Hal nodded. "I watched it happen last year. I couldn't do much to help, either."

"Okay, Iz," I said, blushing, "What do we do about it?"

"I wish I knew." Izzy shook her head. "I'm just seventeen like the rest of you, remember?"

"I have this elective I take with other changelings at Gallows Hill." Brianna leaned back against the padded seat of the booth. "It's supposed to be on maintaining glamour, but it's more like a class in emotional adulting."

"Yeah." Azrael nodded. "I'm in that too. It's self-care, like putting on mental armor."

"Sounds like some folks at our school could use that," Grace mumbled around a mouthful of pizza. "Including me."

"It sounds too personal." Izzy shook her head. "I'm not sure I'd want to be talking about my feelings for a grade. A for everybody."

"It's not like that." Brianna shook her head. "We do yoga, free-writing, and guided meditation. One time we were all tired right after team tryouts, and we took a nap in class like it was kindergarten or something."

"I didn't fall asleep." Azrael tilted his head. "But it was nice to lie down for a minute."

"I think that was the point. We got to stop that day after all the going we did." She sighed. "But anyway, I have a whole book of notes. I could get a copy for you guys. Maybe you can read it in study hall or whatever folks at Hawthorn do during free time."

"Wow, thanks, Brianna." I grinned. "I know that'd help me."

"We still need to talk. I spent most of the summer butting heads with my friends. The point of school break is blowing off steam, a detox before the next year, but it didn't happen for me." Izzy gazed at her hands on the table, letting her fingers curl for a moment. But they flattened again, tips paling.

"Look, I'll go first." I sat up, jostling Ember on my shoulder. She made a sleepy peep before opening her eyes. "This summer I've seen you guys around, but I haven't *seen* you. Our time together felt shallow."

"You've got something there." Cadence nodded. "At school I floundered, but this summer, I waded ankle-deep, like I was scared to get real with my friends."

"I've been so tired." Hal shook his head. "The trips to Boston, the treatments. They helped, but just enough to go to and from them. Even sitting on the beach sapped me. I went to bed to get enough energy to come out for pizza."

"And I can't talk." Izzy stared at the table. "Not about what really bothers me. That place; it's just bizarre. I know we're all extrahumans, the opposite of mundane. But the school stuff you guys talk about?" She shook her head. "Messing's on another planet."

"Oh, Iz, I had no idea." I reached out and put my hand over hers. "I'm sorry."

"You're not a mind reader, Aliyah." Grace dusted crumbs off her hands. "A lifesaver, yeah, because you react fast when it matters. But nobody can know what's in someone else's head, no matter how close they are."

"Hey, that's my line." Izzy gave Grace a wan smile. "I didn't expect it from you, but thanks anyway."

"It's like we were all wrong." I glanced at Cadence then Izzy. "Like we got replaced by body-snatchers all summer."

"You know what?" Azrael leaned around the pitcher so we could see his face. "I felt like that for the last two years before we started our prep schools. I couldn't be the real me. In the group, I mean."

"That was my fault." Izzy shook her head. "I'm sorry. I didn't know how bad that could feel. Like being replaced."

"How could you feel replaced?" Grace blinked.

"Every weekend, Aliyah went on about her awesome roommate, Grace." Izzy looked her in the eye. "That's how. It's not your fault, you're just being yourself. But after Messing, I feel like a friend by proxy, and all last year, you got to have that with her." Lee patted her shoulder.

"You guys are all awesome." I insisted. "None of you are replaceable, including our absent friends."

Nobody said anything after that for a while. Everyone had a bite of pizza or a sip of soda and digested things, both physically and emotionally.

After conversation resumed, the topics changed back to speculation mostly, talking over the activities we'd do once school started. I thought we were out of the woods, at least those of us still sitting at the table.

Faith and Dylan both needed to be looped in on this, and whatever argument Grace had gotten into with him, they'd need to make sure nothing festered. I wasn't sure what had happened, and I didn't find out until a week later because an entirely different can of worms opened for me on the way home.

CHAPTER SIX

"Sorry you missed Gale, girl."

"Peep."

Ember sat on my shoulder, resting her head on top of mine in a fit of what I could only imagine was ennui. I didn't blame her, though. I felt more uneasy than anything else. I wanted to spend more time with Dylan, and not just because he was my friend. He couldn't possibly be okay after whatever had happened outside Engine House. I had no idea how he'd been all summer because he barely left campus except to go to work at Walgreens.

Come to think of it, no one had really seen him outside work besides Hal and Lee. Hawthorn Academy was a big place square-footage wise, despite its few students. Maybe they hadn't spent much time with him either.

I wished I could talk to Logan about Dylan, and wondered what he'd say. As roommates, they'd had each other's backs. But Logan remained on the other side of the country.

"Aliyah, wait up!"

"I'm hearing things." I shook my head, agitating Ember, who turned on my shoulder to look behind me.

"Peep!" She sounded annoyed, not alarmed.

"Yeah, okay, I'm sorry." I kept walking. If someone had followed us, that was all for the best.

Ember let out an honest to goodness roar and flapped her wings, letting go of me to fly back along the way we'd walked.

I'd never seen her angry enough to fly away like that before. I turned to discover what might have set her off.

"Logan?" I froze in place, blinking.

"Yeah, sorry." He shrugged, bags bouncing on his shoulders. The streetlight he stood under was a bluish LED, so his face looked more purple than red under it.

"Meow?" The cat at his feet shimmered in the light. His mercat Doris had glistening silver-gray fur that looked perpetually damp, mottled with charcoal markings.

"Don't apologize, just tell me why you're here." I stepped toward him.

"Well, your grandmother said if I ever needed somewhere to stay," he began, struggling with two rolling suitcases large enough to make my brother Noah jealous.

"Did your parents kick you out?" I gazed at all the luggage, wondering how in the world he'd brought it so far from the train station on his own. That walk was almost ten blocks and uphill half the way.

"Well, no, not exactly. I think I kicked myself out. Maybe." He sighed as one suitcase toppled over on its side. "It's hard to explain."

"That part can wait." I reached down and righted the bag, dragging it beside me. "For now, let's just go talk to Bubbe, okay?"

He nodded. "Sounds like a plan."

I peered at him, counting. He had two messenger bags, one knapsack, and a large rectangular duffel slung over his shoulders. I reached out and snagged the duffel and the knapsack, sharing his burden.

"Where's Ember?" I looked around for my dragonet, then whistled for her.

"Um, here." Logan lifted one of his arms. Ember's little face peeked out from his side.

"Peep?" She blinked, then made puppy dog eyes at me.

"Okay, you can ride on Logan if it's okay with him."

"Yeah, that's fine, Ember. Just hang on, okay?"

"I guess she missed you."

"I missed all this." Logan jerked his chin, indicating the streets of Salem. "And our friends, of course."

"Listen, I'm almost a hundred percent sure Bubbe will let you stay, but you might be downstairs in the animal hospital."

"No problem for me. Dr. Doolittle, remember?" He grinned, but the expression didn't touch his eyes.

"Yeah, I remember." Logan had a special talent for communicating with magical critters. I wasn't sure how it worked, but he'd stopped a gym full of panicked animals from stampeding last year. I'd never seen anything like it.

I wanted to ask him a million questions but didn't. He'd only need to repeat it to Bubbe and probably my parents, so for now, we'd be better off in silence. At least the remaining distance was short.

As we turned the corner into the driveway between my house and Izzy's, she peered out her living room window. Lee joined her momentarily. The two of them waved at us, then Izzy held up a finger. I stopped walking, motioning for Logan to do the same.

"Izzy wants to say hi. Is that okay?"

"That's okay."

As I got up to her house, I noticed Lee's familiar Scratch loping behind them. The two seemed comfortable with each other, which made sense. Izzy wasn't shy around magical critters, having grown up in front of a veterinary office.

"Logan, I wasn't expecting to see you until school started." Lee held out his hand for a shake. "What's up?"

"It's a long story, and I'm tired. Thanks for saying hi. I'm glad to see you guys."

"Do you need anything?" Izzy glanced at all his luggage. "Probably not, but I figured I'd ask."

"You know what?" Logan nodded. "Yeah. There's one thing. Would you mind not telling Dylan I'm here until I'm ready? I'm just too exhausted for now. It'll be at least a couple of days before I'm rested."

"Oh, no problem. I get it; long flights take so much out of people." Lee grinned. "But I bet Dylan will be happy you're here too."

"Thanks." Logan sighed.

"Rough summer?" Izzy raised her eyebrow.

"Like sandpaper." Logan's yawn went on longer than the words that came before it. "Sorry."

"I better take him in. He's still got to talk to Bubbe."

We said goodbye, then walked up the driveway where I rang the bell at the veterinary office. I rarely did that, but it was after hours, and I wanted to let my grandma know someone was here besides family. She answered the door faster than I thought she would.

"Bissel, why did you ring the bell?" Bubbe glanced past me at Logan. "Oh. Hello, Logan. Let me help you with your things."

She didn't ask why he was here but had known he'd show up to accept an offer given nearly a year earlier. I wasn't surprised. My family's kind of big on helping.

I followed them in through the waiting room behind the counter and then past the door to the back. Doris padded behind Logan, keeping close to his heels. Across from the kitchen, Bubbe stopped. She opened a door, one I'd never seen her use in my presence.

"Isn't that the controlled substances closet?" I blinked.

"In a manner of speaking." Bubbe gave us a half-grin. "It's controlled, and there are substances inside, but it's not for medication. Have a look."

We peered through the doorway. The room shouldn't have fit in the hallway between the two examination rooms on either side, but it was bigger on the inside, like Hawthorn Academy's campus. Even so, it was a relatively small space.

"It's a bedroom?" I gave Bubbe a sidelong glance. "But why?"

"Bissel, you knew our house was built at the same time as your school. They're connected in many ways."

"Whatever the reason, I'm glad." Logan seemed to deflate, as though he were far more exhausted than he'd let on earlier.

"You can stay here for as long as you need."

"Thanks. Not too long, though. School will start soon." Logan shuffled through the open door, dragging the one suitcase Bubbe left him with behind him, then he set it aside. "I'll see about staying on campus for school breaks."

Bubbe cleared her throat. "It costs extra, and in the past, students in your *situation* have run into resistance on that front."

"I understand." Logan turned, glancing back at us. I passed him the duffel bag, and he took it but shook his head. "For now, I just need to rest."

"Of course." Bubbe nodded as she passed him another bag. "The kitchen's across the hall. If you're hungry or thirsty in the night, help yourself to snacks. Use the paper plates and the utensils with them; that way everything's kosher. The bathroom is next door to the kitchen."

"You're a lifesaver." Logan took the luggage I'd carried, heaping it in a pile near the door on his side.

"I'll wake you for breakfast tomorrow morning, okay?"

"Meow." Doris head-butted my shin, then walked past Logan into the room.

"If it's okay with Doris, it's okay with me. See you tomorrow, Aliyah. And thanks again, Dr. Morgenstern."

He closed the door, leaving us in the hall. I glanced at my grand-mother, wondering what she'd meant by students in the past in Logan's situation. Mom had stayed here over a summer while at Hawthorn, but I assumed she'd been the only one. I opened my mouth to ask for more details, but Bubbe shook her head.

"Yeah, I know. It's late, and he needs rest. I just want to help."

"That breakfast invitation was a good start. It's waffle day, right?"

"Right." I turned toward the back stairs that led up to our apart-ment on the second and third floors of the building. "Thanks, Bubbe. I love you."

"I love you too."

I headed up the stairs, remembering how last year when my solar magic started coming in, I'd despaired at the top of them. This time around, my concern was for someone else. It was a different sort of burden, so I expected it to feel lighter, but it didn't.

Logan Pierce was in serious trouble. Nobody could have guessed how much, either.

CHAPTER SEVEN

"Waffles!" I hollered down the stairs because Ember kept tugging on my shirt, trying to keep me from leaving the kitchen. I wanted to fetch Logan, but she had berries on the brain. "Waffles up here! Get them while they last!"

"Fat chance." Noah slapped his hand over his mouth because he said them *to* me instead of *at* me.

My brother held grudges like superglue. I turned, trying to counter his pessimism about the availability of delicious waffle-y goodness, but discovered the truth. The waffle batter was almost all gone.

"No way! Waffles!" Logan nearly knocked me over, dashing through the door. He was a picky eater, but I knew from Sunday breakfasts on campus that this was one of his favorite foods.

I let Ember continue pulling me away from the door for safety's sake. Good thing, too. Doris was hard on Logan's heels and would have tripped me in an unfortunate direction if I hadn't moved in time.

I lived in an almost literal zoo, but I wouldn't have had it any other way.

Logan dashed around the counter, skidding to a stop in front of the waffle iron and the bowl beside it. He opened it and ladled batter onto the iron. He closed it, flipping after it buzzed, then got his waffle out just as it turned golden brown.

"I think I can get another half out of this." He held up the bowl, tilting it to scrape the bottom with the ladle. Sure enough, Logan was right.

It was only then that I noticed Noah snickering, and not in a kind way, either.

"What's so funny?" I turned, putting my hands on my hips and glaring like a basilisk.

Noah gazed straight past me, of course, still ignoring me. His attention was focused on Logan Pierce.

"It's just," Noah put his hand over his mouth, lifting his pinky, face turning red, "your shirt."

"Oh, no." Logan hung his head, staring down at the picture and caption emblazoned on his t-shirt.

I blinked, shaking my head so hard anybody watching might have thought I had water in my ear. But I didn't. I was just that surprised.

"Gray Fullbuster is my husbando?" Noah raised his eyebrow. "Not the attire I expected from you."

"It's Elanor's." Logan shook his head again. "Sort of. It was her gag gift last Christmas. I didn't realize it was with my pajamas. She must've snuck it in there before...I mean, I don't know."

"Oh, my God." Noah whipped out his phone. "This is too funny. We've got to take a selfie and send it right now. She'll laugh her ass off."

"You'll do no such thing, Noah." Mom stood in her office doorway, arms crossed over her chest. "Ease off, and no contacting Elanor beyond social media likes until I say so. Especially not about her brother."

"Okay?" Noah blinked.

Mom didn't usually forbid him from anything. Most of the time, I was the one she got strict with. That rarity gave her words more impact, so he listened and put the phone back in his pocket.

"Thanks, Mrs. Morgenstern." Logan set the ladle and bowl back on the counter. "I'm trying to keep my head down."

"It'd be best for you to stay away from campus too, then." Mom crossed her arms over her chest. "At least for the time being. Stick to this building and the backyard. I know that sounds boring but better safe than sorry. And keep our guest's presence a secret. Am I clear here, Noah? Aliyah?"

"Yeah, Mom." I nodded.

"Crystal." Noah sighed. "He's 007 or whatever until you say so."

That's when I noticed Logan had trembled so much he'd dripped the last few drops of batter on the floor, and the half-section inside the iron had gone uncooked. I couldn't get on Noah's case since he'd done nothing wrong, but I needed an outlet for all the tension, so I went to work tidying up.

After snagging a paper towel, I closed the waffle iron before wiping the floor so Logan wouldn't slip. The iron buzzed, and I flipped it for him. I retrieved the bowl and ladle, bringing them to the sink. Finally, I tossed the dirty paper towel into the trash under the counter.

"No need to bang around, Aliyah, geez." Noah rolled his eyes.

"So, now you're talking to me? Because you don't like how I cleaned the kitchen?" I rinsed my hands briskly. "After ribbing my friend over a t-shirt."

My face heated, the anger I'd tried to channel rising again. So did my hands in the water running over them. I checked the faucet. Cold. That meant my temper was about to cause a magical outburst. Not a good look.

"Settle down, Aliyah." Logan got his half-waffle out of the iron, placing it on the plate with the other one. "I'm okay. Got my big boy pants on."

"Okay. As long as you're all right." I took a deep breath and let it out slowly, then one more for good measure.

"I'm fracking sorry, okay?" Noah turned his back and sauntered toward the living room with his half-eaten plate of berry- and syrup-drizzled waffles.

"Peep." Ember landed on my shoulder, nuzzling my face. That

meant she smeared it with strawberries, of course. She'd been sneaking them again.

"I look like I've been snogging a vampire now, don't I?" I sighed.

"You're not wrong." Logan grabbed the fork and knife from the cup next to the stack of plates on the counter. "Hey, where's the syrup?"

"Hold on, I'll get it." I reached into the cabinet to grab the bottle. Once I held it out to Logan, I realized my mistake.

"I don't think so." He shook his head at the bottle of ketchup.

We had a laugh at that, thank goodness. The tension had to break somehow. I wondered about his issues with his parents and the reason he'd left, but there was only one way to find out why.

"So, tell me about that shirt. It looks like anime. What's it from?" I pulled a chair out at the table in the dining room, nodding at it.

"It's from an anime called *Fairy Tail*. We binged it together at the beginning of the summer." Logan took the seat I offered, setting his plate down.

"Sounds cool. Who's the character?" I sat beside him, spooning strawberries on my waffles.

"So, this guy." Logan gestured at the shirt with his fork, "Gray Full-buster, does ice magic. And this girl with water magic gets a totally insane crush on him. Because I'm a water magus and Elanor ships just about everything in the universe—" He took a huge bite of waffle.

"I get it." I grinned. "Her OTP for you is with a fictional ice magus."

"Right." He nodded, pushing pieces of waffle through the syrup on his plate. "Because she's Elanor." He shrugged.

"Which means?" I raised my eyebrow.

"She relates everything to herself, and she's queer." Logan stared at his food. "So naturally, all her shipping is gay."

"Makes sense."

We enjoyed our waffles, talking about silly things Doris and Ember had done over the summer. Some were little habits they'd formed or tricks they'd learned. Since Doris was a mercat, some of those were the opposite of what most people would expect from a feline.

"She stopped sleeping in the kitchen sink after that."

"I didn't even know you could put garbage disposals on timers." I giggled. "But I'm seventeen, and this isn't a smart home. What do I know?"

"Yeah, I guess." Logan shrugged, changing the subject. "I avoid the kitchen too most of the time. We've got a conservatory, like an indoor greenhouse. I used to take care of all the plants in there until Hawthorn. I missed my philodendron all last year if you can believe it."

"Totally." I nodded. "I bet they'd let you have a plant on campus. The lights are solar, so it would do okay in there, right?"

"I should've thought of that." He dragged his fork through dregs of syrup on his plate. "But I'm not sure how I would've brought Benny on the plane, anyway."

He named his plant Benny? How adorable.

Of course, the Evil Inside Voice would pick one of Logan's glum moments to insult something endearing. I finished the last of my strawberries, trying to think of some safe topic to break the silence. Logan managed on his own.

"I wonder how Zeke handles being on campus if all the lights are solar? He's a vampire, but he lives there. How do you think that works?"

"I'm not sure how vampires work physiologically, but I do know a thing or two about solar magic." I held my hand out, palm up. "I'm going to conjure some solar energy right now. Check it out. Once I get it going, hold your hand over it and tell me how it feels."

I focused, calling the magic I'd tried banning myself from the year before. Bubbe had practiced with me three days a week all summer, and it showed. My hand filled with light as I kept a picture in my head, an idea of how that type of sunlight felt.

"It's soft somehow." Logan grinned. "Like an easy afternoon stroll."

"Right." I gave him a smile with my nod. "Because I'm calling it while relaxed. And it's solar energy, not real sunlight. Bubbe explained it as something we conjure from feelings of what sunlight means to us."

"So, vampires who were solar magi could conjure their magic

still?"

"Possibly? For the older ones, it's probably not easy to think kindly of the sun."

"Would they get burned?" Logan studied the side of his index finger and the small scar from the fire in our first lab last year.

"I don't know. Bubbe says vampiric magi get hungry after conjuring. But anyway, that's why vampires can go to the Seelie side of the Under. There's solar energy there, but it's the Sidhe Queen's magic, not the sun. Does that make any sense?"

"Sort of." Logan leaned back in his chair. "I have a million more questions about it, though."

"Better ask at the library once school starts. I just told you everything I know."

"That's fair." He nodded.

"I was wondering something too." I watched him spoon strawberries on his plate, then mix them with the syrup.

"Hmm?" Logan glanced up. The expression he wore reminded me of how he'd looked in Creatives, thinking of something to draw.

"When do you think you'll talk to your family?" The misty quality on his face evaporated like lifting fog.

"Never." He stared back at his plate. "My parents said I'm not one of them anymore, so I guess we can't talk. I'm out. If it wasn't for Bubbe and the nice lady at the airport who changed my ticket, I'd be on the streets in Vegas alone." He dropped his fork against the edge of the ceramic, all interest in the fruit gone. "Why did you ask that?"

"Because things come up." I closed my eyes, imagining my mother down in Providence, testifying against her own brother. "Does it have to be your whole family? What about Elanor?"

"That's up to her, but I'm not holding my breath." Logan's deep sigh reinforced his declaration. "She'll probably just cut me off. They do an awful lot for her."

"So, you don't think this can be fixed?"

"I've tried all my life to fix it." Logan stared into my eyes. Usually, he was thoughtful and caring, a quietly sensitive soul, but this time, his gaze was pure adamantine. "They have to take the first step, and even then." His jaw tightened. "Even if they come with an apology, I still might say no."

"Why?" I blinked, unable to imagine not forgiving anyone in my family. But no two families were the same, a lesson I'd seen demonstrated outside the classrooms over and over at Hawthorn Academy.

"Because I have to pick something, Aliyah. Choose a way to handle this." Logan's eyes clouded like a storm rolling over the bay. "I'm never what they want, and every time I get close, they change the rules on me."

"I don't understand?" I reached across the table, taking Logan's hand. "But I want to."

"It's always been that way." He shook off my grip. "Being a Pierce is conditional, like living in a maze of 'if-onlies.' If only you were a triple-threat like Elanor. If only you were a showman like your father. If only you were like the telekinetic kid in that other family's act."

"That stuff doesn't matter, Logan." I turned my hand over, placing it flat on the table. "Not to your friends. We think you're awesome. And grades don't lie. You're top of the class."

"My parents didn't get the memo." He snorted. "My heart can't take any more. They either love me or they don't. Nobody turns out the way their parents expect. Going to school with all of you last year taught me that much."

"You're right." I nodded. "Just don't be surprised if you have to face them again. There's a reason 'absence makes the heart grow fonder' is an old adage. And some people's ideas about fondness aren't all sunshine and roses."

"You sound like somebody's grandma."

"Thanks." I reached out again, offering my hand instead this time. Logan eyed it for a moment, then took it. "Even though I talk like an old babushka, I'm your friend. And I'm not going anywhere, no matter how many plants you've got in your dorm room, husbando shirts you wear, or mercats you adopt off the streets."

Logan didn't say anything, but he didn't have to. Neither of us did. That's the way friendship is. And for about a week, things went smoothly for him.

CHAPTER EIGHT

Six days after he arrived, Mom invited us into her office to read a message for Logan.

"It seems your transfer student arrives today." Mom lifted the privacy screen on her monitor so Logan could see it. "Headmaster Hawkins has requested your presence on campus to help him with housing orientation."

"Housing orientation?" I asked, "Is the new guy a fire magus or something? Why would anyone need orientation to inhabit a dorm room?"

"I don't know." Logan bent to peer at the screen. "I guess I'll find out. Or rather, *we* will." He grinned, then pointed at the message.

"Oh!" I blinked. "Headmaster Hawkins let you have a plus one?"

"Looks like it," he said. "So you get to visit campus before the school year starts after all."

"Peep!" Ember leaped off my shoulder, soaring through the air. I felt her excitement since magi with a familiar bond often shared emotions with our critters.

"They're letting me move in, so I'll tell Bubbe I don't need the room anymore." Logan straightened. "I'll go pack my stuff."

Mom tilted her head, gazing at him. "Remember, you can stay here on breaks or weekends if you need to get off-campus."

"Okay." He nodded and his eyes brightened, expression dreamy.

I knew him well enough to guess he didn't think he'd need it. For better or worse, optimism remained part of Logan's mental landscape, despite the crap his parents had heaped on him all summer.

"There's more information here for you, Logan. From the headmaster." Mom turned toward the printer, pulling the freshly ejected sheet from its tray. "Let's have a look."

"Thanks, Mrs. Morgenstern."

Since my friend was in good hands, I headed upstairs, packing one of my suitcases with things I wouldn't need until school started. I could put them in the room I'd share with Grace a week later. I glanced at the trusty old communication orb, my lifeline on the offline campus to Izzy and Cadence. At Hawthorn, it was forbidden and had gotten me in serious trouble last year. Should I bring it and risk more probation, or leave it behind?

Getting caught with a contraband magipsychic device might get me suspended or even expelled. I'd start this year on disciplinary probation. But the orb saved two lives last year, maybe three, I wasn't sure. Leaving it behind would be nerve-wracking.

I'd been all but promised more trouble on campus by the outgoing mean girl, who'd enlisted her younger sister and my ex to continue harassing me. I knew but had no proof that she'd been behind a magisupremacist hate crime. Said trouble would extend to my friends from town.

In October, the Hawthorn Academy campus would see the most diverse group of students in its entire history during extramurals. Our school's bylaws excluded much, including vampire students, a ban Messing Academy and Gallows Hill didn't share. Would I be putting this diverse group of extrahumans at risk if I didn't bring the orb?

But Izzy and Cadence were on their school's teams, so they'd be on campus with me. We could work together to make another orb in an emergency, possibly with faculty permission. One of the events was a magipsych fair, during which students could make devices like the orb. Maybe the risk was less than I imagined. I packed more mundane tools for protesting hate instead.

The Vamp Lives Matter t-shirt I'd stolen from Noah last year went into the suitcase, and another with the Night Creatures' latest album art on it. I threw in an Ultimate Shifter League shirt and one bearing the logo for Monarch Motion Pictures, a faerie-run indie film company. If I wanted to fight back against discrimination, I'd do it wholeheartedly. And with style, I thought as I added the houndstooth leggings that looked particularly cute with the first shirt.

Headmaster Hawkins shared my sentiments, but I wasn't as sure about the rest of the faculty, so I surrounded the bundle with menstrual supplies, underwear, bras, and cozy socks. A box of Auntie's Anti-cramp tea rounded out the packing. Even if somebody checked it, which could happen to students on probation, they'd only see comfort items. Some folks were still squeamish about looking through stuff like that.

The next order of business was adding accessories, fussy little things like necklaces and scarves I rarely bothered with in town. Noah wouldn't pick them out for me this year. He hadn't spoken to me since that accidental instance on waffle morning. I figured he wasn't likely to any time soon.

"How do people even figure this stuff out?" I shook my hands, one of which held a blue choker and the other an orange teardrop pendant.

"Peep?" Ember tilted her head to the left and then the right. She blinked a few times, stared at the tunics I had hanging on the closet door, then back at the necklaces. "Peep peep."

My dragonet swooped down, snagged the orange teardrop pendant from my hand, and dropped it in the suitcase. People weren't necessary to make fashion choices, apparently.

"Hopefully, you've got good taste in jewelry." I shrugged, placing the choker back in the box on my dresser.

"Want help?" Logan stood in the doorway, Doris brushing past his legs and into the room. She leaped into my suitcase, turned in a circle, and made herself comfortable on top of the lingerie bag. "Picking outfits is something I did to get out of more performing."

"Yeah, sure." I shrugged, smiling at the purring mercat.

"Doris does that to me all the time, gets in the bags I'm packing as if I'd forget to bring her." Logan chuckled. "Where's that string of freshwater pearls? The ones you wore with the pink dress on Valentine's Day?"

"You think I'll need those?"

"Yeah. You can wear them with all those dresses." He waved his hand at the garment bag on my bed, which contained the mint green dress I'd worn to parents' night last year along with a sample from Ambersmith Fashions Grace had dropped off for me last month.

"Okay. What about scarves?"

"No clue." Logan shrugged. "Nobody wears them in Vegas unless they're hiding a hangover. Let's not get drunk at any ragers while on probation, okay?"

We laughed.

"Guess I'll just bring the most comfortable ones."

I grabbed a yellow and white floral chiffon, then a silky emerald green. On top of that, I added a knobbly woolen one for when it got colder. My gloves and coat went in on top since, while I wouldn't need them in September, I would want to be warm on the way home on weekends in November.

"Oh, no." Logan sighed. "I left my winter stuff in Vegas."

"Maybe Elanor will bring it."

"I don't know." He leaned against the doorframe.

"You messaged her about Benny though, right?"

"No. Not yet." Logan looked at his feet, then at Doris in the suitcase. "After I've moved in on campus, I'll send her a message from the headmaster's office. It's safer if they don't know I'm here."

"Safer?" I blinked.

From his parents, of course.

"Come on, Queen Doris." Logan didn't answer. "Time to get out of there."

The mercat stood up, stretching each limb one at a time. Eventually, she stepped out of the suitcase, but she took her sweet time. I didn't mind; it gave me space to breathe. For whatever reason, I'd gotten nervous about going to campus.

You should be. Your friend's gone renegade from his influential family. Do you honestly think they'll let it lie? What was on that paper your mother didn't let you see?

"Hey, Logan?"

"Hmm?" He already looked exhausted.

"Are you meeting this new student on the way in?" Ember perched on my headboard, shuffling from side to side with her wings partly out like a canary in a room full of cats.

"Yeah, I am." He shrugged. "Why?"

"Do you want to bring Izzy with us, just for the walk to find the door?" I kept my eyes on my dragonet. The suggestion had a profound effect on her behavior. The shuffling stopped, and she folded her wings.

"Are you getting a funny feeling?"

"Yes." Ember echoed my answer with a peep.

"Okay, then."

I grabbed the suitcase and the garment bag. Once we said goodbye to my parents, I headed down the back stairs with Logan and we got his luggage from the hallway in Bubbe's office. In the waiting room on our way out, we ran into Eston, one of our classmates.

"Logan?" Eston blinked. "What are you doing here?"

"Just heading to campus. I'm mentoring the new student in our year."

"I mean, *here*." Eston waved his hand, indicating Bubbe's office. "At the Morgenstern's."

"Why are *you* here?" Logan pulled his suitcase along behind him, heading toward the exit.

He's trying to change the subject. Failing miserably at it, too.

"Familiar license. I'm from New Hampshire, so it's just a medium drive for me. But you, you're—"

"In town early. I know." Logan's laugh came out flatter than usual. "Funny, running into you here."

Coincidental, perhaps.

"They've been looking all over for you, man. Watch out."

"Okay." Logan pushed the door open, beckoning to me with his chin. "Gotta go."

"Aliyah, watch out for him. This isn't good."

Get more information.

"How? What do you mean?" I tried stammering out more questions because it's rare that I agree with the Evil Inside Voice. But outside the door, I heard Logan calling to Izzy in the driveway. "Oops, gotta go, Eston. Sorry."

"Just be careful." Eston headed toward the door Bubbe held open for him, then looked back over his shoulder. "See you next week."

"Yeah, see you." The door closed behind me.

CHAPTER NINE

Out in the driveway, it was almost too bright. The sun beat down on us, without even a single wispy cloud in the sky to dim its rays. Of all the times to forget my sunglasses. I squinted, shuffling along the gravel and hoping I wouldn't trip.

I didn't, which was a good thing because Izzy stood at the end of the driveway. She had a bungee cord with her, which confused me until she took two bags off of Logan's shoulders and set them on top of his rolling suitcase, securing them with the stretchy cord.

"How did you know I needed that?" Logan scratched his head.

"Psychic. But really, I watched you come up the driveway last week, remember? Shoulder injuries are not a good look."

"Thanks." Logan grinned as Doris headbutted Izzy's shin. "We're all nervous and wondering if there's anything to it."

"I hear you." Izzy nodded, reaching into the satchel she always wore slung on one hip. It contained her tarot cards, the ones she'd use to get a little extra information about whatever situation arose.

She pulled out a card, then frowned.

Trouble, of course.

"Who are you fighting with, Logan?" She turned the Two of Wands around.

"Um. My parents? Maybe my whole family."

"Would they call the police on you for any reason?"

"I'm not sure? It happened once when I was ten, but I never understood why."

"Maybe we should go through the fence behind my house." On Hawthorne Street behind Logan, I saw a police cruiser drive past more slowly than usual. "Come on up the driveway now."

"Peep!" Ember swooped behind Logan, diving at him until he headed back in the direction I'd indicated.

We squeezed past my parents' car, heading toward the gate in the fence. I opened it and we hustled through, Izzy closing it behind us. We had to lift the suitcases instead of rolling them because the path was a series of stepping stones with gravel between them. All the way in the back right corner of the yard, a large jasmine bush stood sentry in front of the hole in the fence. Noah and I had thought it our secret for ages, but a few years ago, after my brother bonded with Lotan, we realized Bubbe knew.

Lotan tried to go exploring, which was how we discovered unaccompanied critters couldn't get through. A magical ward banning lone animals covered the hole in the fence. Bubbe exercised some of her boarders and patients recovering from various injuries out here, so that made sense. I knew how to take it down because we'd practiced wards in Lab last year. All I needed was to match and banish the element making the magic barrier.

As I conjured my solar magic, Logan spoke.

"What did Eston say? After I left?"

"He said to be careful, and I'm taking his warning seriously." I snapped my fingers, banishing the fire and shutting off the ward. "But it's also that card, the Two of Wands. It's meant the police before in Izzy's readings, and I just saw a squad car drive down Hawthorne Street."

"I don't get it." Logan shook his head, ducking under the shrubbery I held aside for him. "They told me to leave. I'm almost an adult already. And they didn't know where I went."

"Hold on." Izzy drew another card, the Page of Wands reversed. "Half the time, this card signifies Noah. Maybe he ratted you out."

I'm too ashamed to repeat the string of words that came out of my mouth right then, but the Evil Inside Voice had a good long laugh at them. I was angry enough that some flowers on the jasmine bush wilted.

"Chill out! We're in the middle of a big getaway, remember?" Izzy patted my shoulder, helping me focus enough to turn down the wattage on my solar magic.

Once we got to the other side of the fence, I put the wards back up. We headed down the walkway beside the Peabody Essex Museum. Since the rest of our route traversed pedestrian-only terrain, I relaxed. Cars couldn't go on Essex Street, and conventional technology didn't work there. Most of the Salem PD didn't have access to magipsychic tech at that point, and only one officer was an extrahuman.

Oh, look, it's Pirate Day. Lovely.

The Evil Inside Voice's commentary wasn't welcome, but it wasn't wrong either. A banner hung from poles set up beside the Peabody Essex Museum, bearing an old-timey message: Ye Olde Salem Pirate Festival, 8-8 today!

Immediately after making the turn, we dodged clusters of puffy-shirted people and began scanning the buildings for Hawthorn Academy's migrating entrance. Its location varied every twenty-four hours as part of campus security, and it figured that on the day we were in a hurry, we didn't find it on the first few tries.

"What's the rush, you guys?" Azrael Ambersmith jogged to keep up with us.

Logan panted. "Just trying to get to school."

"It's way down there by the Italian restaurant." He pointed past a gaggle of pirates. Yes, people in pirate garb walked down, along, across, and around Essex Street. "Are you avoiding someone? Do you need help?"

"Yeah, help would be good." Izzy nodded. "Can you throw a glamour on our pal Logan here? He needs to blend in."

"Okay." Azrael cracked his knuckles. "What do you want, pirate garb?"

"Um, I don't know?" Logan shrugged, blinking owlishly. The crowd and the chaos were getting to him, then. He needed help.

I glanced at the festive folk, noticing that most of them wore garb more akin to Renaissance Faire attire than Pirates of the Caribbean. This meant plenty of enormous face-concealing hats instead of bandannas and eyepatches.

"Yeah, pirate." I nodded. "Go for it."

"Sure." Azrael concentrated, then tapped Logan on the shoulder the way he had when we were kids playing tag.

A moment later, Logan's clothes sort of fluffed out. His shirt grew long, frilly sleeves, and his Bermuda shorts became pantaloons. A flick of Az's wrist added a leather vest and a sword belt to the imaginary ensemble. The glamour did nothing to mask his features, but the feather-bedecked tricorn hat perched on his head helped with that.

"Nice timing, Az." Izzy jerked her thumb. "Check it out." A police officer on a bicycle pedaled slowly past us down Essex Street as we made it to the restaurant he'd mentioned earlier.

"Oh no, I did not just help you evade the cops." Az paled, eyes widening in horror. "I'm gonna get in so much trouble if my dad ever finds out."

"It's okay." She pulled a card but didn't show us. "It's a bogus reason. We won't tell your dad."

"Yeah, Logan's a good kid, I promise." I patted Azrael's shoulder. "He was the valedictorian last year. All we have to do is get him on campus, and everything will be fine."

Logan blushed, shuffling his feet and staring at his boat shoes, which looked like tall leather boots now. Something hit him in the back of the head, knocking the glamoured tricorn hat right off it.

"That shouldn't happen!" Azrael stepped back, blinking and holding his hands up. He wasn't surprised, but scared. "It's glamour."

"Gryphon beats glamour, my fine unfeathered changeling friend." The guy talking was short, slight, and dressed all in black except for the navy blue Hawthorn Academy blazer, to which he'd somehow added silver piping on the seams. His jet-black hair was parted on one side, where a stark white streak covered one of his eyes. "What is this, Dress Like a Pirate Day?"

"Excuse me, who are you?" Izzy crossed her arms over her chest, tapping her foot and glaring at the newcomer.

"Door." He smirked, pointing at himself and then at the thing we sought. "But that's not my name. It's Dorian Spanos. I'm the new guy."

"Why did a gryphon hit me?" Logan rubbed the back of his head. "I kind of need that hat right now."

"Might as well ask why snow falls down instead of up." Dorian sighed, ironically. "So, what are these reasons of yours?"

Before anyone could answer him, the bicycling police officer screeched to a stop beside the group. Azrael froze, except for his hands, which visibly trembled. His face went white as a sheet.

"Logan Pierce?" The officer put down the kickstand and got off the bike. "Show me your ID slowly."

"Oh, no way." Dorian's smile was broad, showing a set of even white teeth.

"Yeah, I'm Logan Pierce. My ID is in my back pocket here. I'm just going to reach for it."

The police officer waited, then checked the piece of plastic Logan handed over. She peered at it, tilting it in the light and watching the sun play on the hologram Nevada put on its state IDs. Apparently, Logan didn't have a driver's license.

"Looks like the real deal." The officer tossed her head, the ponytail under her bike helmet shining ruddily in the sunlight. "You're coming with me, though, Logan. Your parents want you escorted to the airport."

"He's not going to the airport." Headmaster Hawkins strode through the door to Hawthorn Academy, heading directly for our group. "Mr. Pierce is expected at school today. His tuition is paid in full for the year, and he's got work to do here."

"I'm sorry, Headmaster, but his parents reported him missing and said they had reason to believe he'd be in Salem."

"His parents are mistaken." Headmaster Hawkins held out a piece of paper, handing it to the officer. "I've got an agreement he signed to mentor a student at my school, beginning today."

"Oh?" The police officer raised her eyebrow, stepping back so sharply her ponytail bobbed. She glanced back at the ID. "He's seventeen. They didn't tell us that."

"Have a look." He smiled mildly. "It's notarized and everything."

I blinked because notarization requires all signatories to be present in the room with the Notary Public. As far as I remembered, Logan had signed his document in Nevada after receiving it via certified mail.

I managed to catch a glimpse of the paper as he passed it and noticed its date was last week and the notary my father.

"It seems to be in order, but I'll have to show it to my lieutenant. Hang on a moment." She got out her phone and tried taking a picture, then shrugged and laughed at herself. It didn't work because this was Essex Street.

I looked for Azrael since he might know some way to take and convey a picture to the police station, but he'd faded into the crowd.

"Let's make this easier." Headmaster Hawkins said. "Why don't I bring the document to the station? If your lieutenant thinks it's not in order, we'll rectify it together."

"That works." She nodded. "Assuming there's supervision for the students on campus while you're away."

"Several of the faculty and staff are here preparing for the start of classes. Mr. Pierce's professor is one of them. Will that do?"

"Yes." She nodded. "Once the students enter the school, we can go."

We said goodbye to Izzy, then Logan and I headed through the entrance, along with Dorian, whose mischievous gryphon was perched on his shoulder. Once the door closed behind us, the new transfer student leaned against it and laughed so hard I thought he'd fall over.

"Holy shit." Dorian grinned at Logan, wheezing in a breath between clenched teeth. "You're not what I expected at all. This is gonna be awesome. Mentored by a student who fought the law. And won."

"Some people think that's a bad thing." Logan blinked.

"Not me. Didn't they tell you I'm a transfer from the Academy?" Dorian waggled his eyebrows. "I'm starting on probation."

"No. They did not tell me that." Logan's voice was deadpan. He'd been caught off-guard and out of his element.

I had his back. "Yeah, we're a couple of miscreants, for sure." I elbowed Logan in the ribs. "I'm on probation too."

"Sick." Dorian nodded. "When do we get food in this place?"

"Next time's lunch, in half an hour. What room are you in? We can put your stuff away."

"I just have this bag." Dorian peered at all the luggage. "You look like you overpacked, man. You too, fellow probationary student."

"Yeah, it's a bad habit." I shook my head. Of all the times to pack more like Noah than me. "What can you do?"

"Anyway, I'm on the third floor. I guess everyone in our year is, right?"

"Yup." I pulled the suitcase behind me toward the stairs. "It's voice-activated, like an escalator except magical."

"Aliyah, what are you doing?" Logan leaned toward my ear, whispering as we walked.

"Speaking miscreant, I guess." I shrugged. "Just come up one step." I beckoned to the new guy.

"Right." Once he got on, I spoke the words "third floor," and the staircase started moving.

On the way up, Logan gripped my elbow tightly, like a lifeline over the side of the boat in stormy seas. I'm not sure what had him so ill at ease. The headmaster had solved the police problem. But if his parents had called to report him missing when they'd actually kicked him out, things were not okay.

I couldn't miss the way my friend kept staring at the new student. Maybe he found Dorian intimidating. Or maybe he worried that his parents had been right all along, and he shouldn't have accepted the offer to be a student mentor. That he was out of his depth here.

Or it's something else. You certainly don't know everything.

I shrugged off the snark from the Evil Inside Voice. Either way, he'd need help. Too-cool-for-school Dorian Spanos was a wild card. I'd had enough trouble with one of those last year, and now one of my friends had to deal with the 2.0 version. Grace would need a heads-up. She'd texted the day before about having a plan for the year ready to go.

As it turned out, an entirely different set of difficulties loomed on the horizon for our group.

CHAPTER TEN

We escorted Dorian down the hall toward the room he'd share with Eston. Even though Alex remained at Hawthorn Academy, he'd room with one of the first-years. I had no idea how Eston felt about any of that. Usually, he reserved his thoughts and opinions for his girlfriend Kitty. Eston was the quiet type.

"Are you going to unpack that?" Logan pointed at the still-closed duffel bag on the floor.

"Nah. I'll save that for later." Dorian laughed as he sauntered back out the door. His gryphon tilted her head, blinking at us with a soft caw. "I'll hang with you guys while you stow your stuff, then we can get some grub."

"Okay, I guess." Logan shrugged.

"Is that cool with your girlfriend here?" Dorian waggled his eyebrows.

"Friend who happens to be a girl."

"That's fine." I snorted, imagining Izzy and all her protestations about boys.

"Cool-cool." Dorian nodded, his smirk blossoming into a genuine smile.

"Let's drop your stuff off first, Logan." I offered. "You shouldn't have to lug all those bags to my room and back."

"Peep!" Ember crept out from under my hair, shaking herself free. After that, she stretched her wings, yawning. I kept walking toward the room I shared with Grace.

"Oh, no way!" Dorian smiled. "You've got a dragonet?"

"Yup, one of two here." I shrugged. Ember trilled playfully.

Logan nodded. "My roommate has the other one."

"Will we see him today?" Dorian picked up his pace. It wasn't always easy for my shorter friends to match my stride, and the new kid was no exception.

"I'm not sure," Logan said. "Dylan's a workaholic with two jobs, so he might not be around."

"Oh, Logan. I meant to tell you something about Dylan." I glanced at Dorian. "Maybe it's personal."

"How's something maybe personal?" Dorian blinked. "Either it is or it isn't, right?"

"Things can be totally complicated around here. You get used to it." I gave Dorian a half-smile, then headed back into the hall, closing the door behind me.

"Oh, boy." He rolled his eyes. "Drama llama ding-dong."

"You can say that again," Logan muttered.

"Meow." Doris glared up at Dorian as though daring him to repeat himself. Sometimes, the mercat reminded me of the reference librarian at the Salem Public Library.

"I won't. Are we cool, Doris?" Dorian leaned forward, peering at the feline as he walked. His gryphon leaned forward too, head bobbing. "Mercy's sorry about the hat earlier. She didn't know she'd cause such a ruckus."

"Yeah, I think she's okay with you now." Logan shrugged. "The two of us are kind of on the serious side. And here we are."

Logan put his hand on the flat wooden panel beside the door to his room. The lock clicked and he opened it, pushing his way inside. The lights came on as Dorian and I followed Logan in. He helped, lifting the largest suitcase to the top of Logan's bed, but he winced a little while doing it, like something twinged or pinched.

"At least it's obvious which one is yours." Dorian jerked his thumb at Dylan's unmade bed. A beat-up acoustic guitar sat there, partially draped by a sheet. "For a workaholic, his housekeeping's kinda sloppy."

"Not usually." I closed the door behind me. The last thing I wanted was Dylan to walk in on us talking about him. "I hope he's okay. He had some kind of argument with Grace outside Engine House last week. He came in and sat for maybe five minutes, but I haven't seen him since."

"Really?" Logan dropped his knapsack, then headed toward Dylan's side of the room. He peered at the desk and into the trash can and looked beside the door. "Well, he's been here today. And he's wearing his work shoes now, so he must be on a shift at one job or the other."

Dorian raised his eyebrows, watching Logan intently, and said nothing. I wondered what he thought about all this. Pretty much all the students in our year erred on the side of kindness, and I wasn't sure yet whether Dorian would be on board with it. Time would tell.

"Well, I'll get Doris's stuff out, then we can go to the cafeteria." Logan opened his knapsack, producing a plethora of cat accessories.

Hawthorn Academy supplied food and water for the magical critters, but anything else had come from the students. Despite Logan's parental issues, Doris had been taken care of, at least. But I expected nothing less from Logan. For all I knew, he raided the feline accessories from his family's show.

"All set." Logan brushed his hands off, then headed toward the door to open it. "Everybody out."

"I'm just gonna drop this off in my room, no need to unpack." I stopped two doors down from Logan's.

When I opened the door, Dorian stopped to hold it open. I collapsed the handle on the suitcase, then pushed it under the bed. After that, I turned to find him staring at the wall over Grace's bed, which was adorned with the usual Hawthorn Academy wooden carvings but partially covered by her posters.

"Your roommate's into K-Pop?"

"Yup." Ember added a peep of her own. She liked Grace's music.

"I'm sorry."

Something about Dorian threw me off. It seemed like he was hiding something or trying too hard, or both, but Logan had to help him. Mentorship was part of everything else he'd have to deal with, and his plate was already piled high. I'd have to get along with Dorian somehow, but I also had to stand up for my friend.

"I'm not." I put my hands on my hips, planting my feet. "That's a snobby thing to say."

"Yeah, it was. I shouldn't have said it. Bad inside voice, no biscuit."

Don't get any ideas about talking to me like that, miss.

"I know a little something about unruly inside voices." I snorted. "But be careful. Our year is pretty chill. The third-years, not so much, and I've got no idea what the first-years will be like."

"That's not true." Logan sighed. "We kind of expect a bit of trouble."

"Trouble?" Dorian cracked his knuckles. "What kind?"

Most of my friends would've blinked, stepped back, or otherwise expressed alarm. Not Dorian Spanos. He seemed more intense than chaotic, so I wondered whether he was a daredevil or had a death wish. Either could throw an enormous monkey wrench into practically every social dynamic we'd built last year.

"Mean girl stuff." I shrugged. "There's a downright awful one coming next week. Don't worry, my K-Pop-loving roommate has a plan."

"We should probably tell him about Alex."

"In a while." I headed toward the doorway. "Maybe off-campus, okay?"

"Oh, come on. Now I'm curious." Dorian's voice cracked on the last syllable.

"Don't worry, you'll hear about it." Logan put a hand on his shoulder to escort him away from the door. "Just not here."

"Oh, it's like that, is it?" Dorian tensed, eyes widening until Logan dropped his hand. He swallowed before continuing, "You guys are lucky you can leave campus. The Academy didn't let us do that."

What was all that about, I wonder?

I kept my lips zipped. The silence as we walked down the hallway felt like one of the enormous, wobbly bubbles Cadence had insisted on making all through grade school. They floated along almost impossibly before popping. Anyone in direct proximity got soap in their eyes. I knew better than to tamper with the social equivalent.

"First floor." I activated the staircase as soon as we reached it.

I didn't want to continue the conversation about The Academy. I'd overheard just enough about it through the door of Mom's office. Dorian must've picked up on that because he changed the subject.

"What kind of food do they have here?"

"Just about everything." Logan smiled. "Not every day, but the selection is good, and they rotate things. They're also good with allergies and special diets, that kind of thing."

"The stuff we got over at the Academy was crap." When the stairs stopped, Dorian paced ahead of us, turning around and walking backward. "Sometimes I thought it was dog food."

"Ugh." Logan wrinkled his nose.

"Exactly."

"Look, they have panini." I pointed at the board.

"I'm surprised they're even open." Logan shook his head. "I mean, almost nobody's on campus."

"The headmaster said Luciano and Nurse Smith are." I shrugged. "Those two would mutiny without a decent meal."

"Makes sense," Dorian said, laughing. "So, profs eat the same stuff we do?"

"Yeah, why wouldn't they?" Logan blinked.

"You've probably never been stuck at a crappy school, either of you."

"I've been to them." I sighed. "My mom works in extrahuman education."

"Well, you're right about me." Logan shrugged. "All the schools I went to, the food at least looked good."

"I care more about how it tastes." Dorian stepped up to the counter. "I'm starving."

I got my usual turkey on pumpernickel with avocado, while Logan got ham and Swiss. Dorian ordered two sandwiches, one Italian with provolone and the other roast beef with cheddar. The sandwiches came out so fast they might have been made in the future. Maybe they were. The cafeteria employed Penelope, whose familiar could warp time.

We took our trays to the beverage station, where I got iced tea. Logan went with his usual Sprite. Dorian got a cup and went along the line, putting a little of everything cold in his cup, and I mean everything. He added all the sodas, juice, and even the iced tea.

"What's that?" Logan blinked.

"Beverage roulette." Dorian took a sip, then wrinkled his nose. "You never know if it's going to be good or like this." He took another sip, longer this time.

"Why not dump it out and try again?" Logan asked.

"I made it, now I have to drink it." He shrugged, then headed toward the tables. "Them's the rules."

"Let's sit here." I put my tray at the booth we used last year.

We ate in silence for a few minutes. Dorian must have been hungry because he finished his entire first sandwich. I only managed a quarter of mine.

Something moved, so I turned my head to see what it was, but nothing was there. Logan did the same thing, but Dorian laughed.

"It's just my familiar." He pointed to where I'd seen the movement. "Look up at the light fixture. Mercy likes those."

I made out a shape on the light. It reminded me of how a hawk used the sun for cover, so the prey wouldn't see it before the final dive-bomb. Sure enough, a moment later, Mercy the gryphon plummeted through the air, dipping into the trash can and coming up with a sandwich crust. She fluttered over, perching on the edge of the table with her prize.

Lovely. A trash gryphon. What will young Headmaster Hawkins allow on campus next? Ah, yes. The extrahuman riffraff, including your town friends.

"I'd better read up on gryphons." I stared down my sandwich, nostrils flaring as I resisted snapping back at the Evil Inside Voice. "It's one of the few critters I know little about. They rarely partner with magi."

"Oh, yeah, nobody expected it," Dorian said. "I'm already the odd magus in the family. My familiar was just the latest straw. Hopefully, the fact that Mercy's unconventional won't be the last."

"Are you in trouble with them?" Logan asked flatly.

"Nah, my folks are good people. They just don't know what to do with me. They're psychic. I'd think I was adopted, but I look just like them. Except for this." He indicated the white streak in his hair. "It came in with my magic."

"I know how you feel. I'm the lone introvert in a showbiz family. They love getting in front of people and making spectacles out of themselves. I'd rather sit in a corner and draw."

"Right on." Dorian nodded. "And yet here you are at the school they sent you to."

"They're not happy about me being in Salem now." Logan closed his eyes. "But the tuition's non-refundable at this point."

"Yeah, about that." Dorian leaned on his hand, reminding me of Cadence. "Did they really call the police on you?"

"I guess." Logan shrugged. "News to me. Unpleasant, but that's not exactly new. Tell him, Aliyah."

Dorian blinked and said nothing. He glanced at me, eyes widening.

"He was staying with my grandma because they kicked him out of the house last week." I made a fist against the table. "She offered him a place last year because they didn't want him bonding with Doris. She's apparently not fancy enough for them."

Doris chose that moment to turn on the charm, leaping up on the back of the booth behind Logan and pacing back and forth like the world's glossiest feline tightrope walker. She stared at Dorian the entire time as if daring him to share in the Pierce Family consensus.

"No way." Dorian watched her. "Totally gorgeous."

"Thanks." Logan's face was almost as red as the tomato garnish beside his sandwich.

"So, someone expected their shenanigans." Dorian glanced at my curled hand and then back up again, but at Logan, not me. "What kind of parents call the cops when they gave you the boot?"

Go on and tell the boy his parents are toxic. Evil, even. Make him cry right here in front of his mentee, who already makes him feel awkward.

I closed my eyes and swallowed the fiery diatribe against the entire Pierce family, excluding Logan. This was his story to tell.

"They always treated my sister better than me." Logan cut the crust from his sandwich and tossed it to Mercy, who gobbled it down in moments. "But is that normal? I've got no idea."

"It's not." Dorian and I startled each other by speaking at the same time.

"Jinx, you owe me beverage roulette." Dorian laughed and slapped the table.

"After I finish my sandwich, okay?" I grinned.

"Thanks, guys." Logan stared down at his ham and Swiss, then picked it up and finally took a bite.

Sometimes a well-placed laugh is just as important as a shoulder and an open ear.

A moment later, Lee headed toward us, sauntering over from the food line. He had tomato soup and a side of sweet potato fries on his tray.

"Is this seat taken?" he asked.

"There's always room for another friend." Logan waved his hand, and Dorian scooted over. "Dorian, this is Lee. He's in our year, too."

"Hey." Dorian bobbed his head. "What's up besides the crazy solar light fixtures?"

"The ceiling." Lee grinned. "Anyway, good to meet you."

We went about the business of lunch, the conversation turning academic. Since Dorian was in Professor Luciano's section with Logan and me, we answered most of his questions. If that bothered Lee, he didn't show it. He barely spoke until after we finished our food.

"So, I've been wandering the halls, helping Scratch exercise. And I heard something."

"Couldn't have been ghosts, right?" Dorian glanced around.

"No. Campus is between worlds, so ghosts can't come here." Lee shook his head. "It's music. Apparently, Dylan has a new hobby."

"You mean my roommate?" Logan blinked. "Okay."

"After the umpteenth time I walked past his room, he came out and asked if I'd go see him at the open mic night."

"Oh, yeah." I nodded. "The Witch's Brew has one every Sunday. It's at seven."

"Yeah, that's tonight." Lee twirled the spoon in his empty bowl. "He might appreciate more people rooting for him than little old me."

"I'll be there." I nodded. "With friends from town, hopefully."

"Oh." Logan gazed at the crumbs on his plate. "I probably shouldn't go off-campus. Not unless Headmaster Hawkins says it's safe."

"Huh?" Lee peered at Logan. "Why not?"

"He's avoiding the cops." Dorian grinned. "You should have seen it. They almost arrested him in the middle of Essex Street."

"Even if I can't make it, go with Lee. You'll meet a ton of cool people, Dorian. Including Dylan." Logan got up, snagging his tray. "I should unpack and track down the headmaster. See you all later."

"Wait." I got up. "I can't be on campus without you until school starts, remember?"

"Oh, sorry." Logan paused, his back toward our friends at the table. "I'll walk you out."

"See you guys later!" I waved at Lee and Dorian.

We walked together in silence, dropping off our trays at the dish-washing window. He didn't speak until we got into the vestibule between the lobby and the exit.

"Sorry this is so hard." I reached out and patted his shoulder. Ember landed on mine, then craned her neck toward my friend, peeping softly at him.

"I didn't expect it to be easy, but the police?" He hung his head. Doris trotted over, rubbing her body against his legs. He opened his arms, and she jumped into them.

"Listen, if you need me, send a message out with Lee or Dylan. I'll stop by."

"Thanks." Logan cuddled Doris, who put her paw on his cheek. "I wish I could look on the bright side, but I'm not sure there is one."

"It got Dorian on your side, at least. He seems like a rebel, but now maybe he'll take advice from you?"

"We'll see." He shrugged. "I'll ask the headmaster if you can come to the library this week. I'm bringing Dorian there, so maybe Hawkins will—"

"Maybe I'll what?"

Last year, we would have jumped out of our shoes at the sudden interruption, but we'd gotten used to the headmaster's habit of randomly and suddenly appearing on campus.

"Allow Aliyah to come and go freely to campus. To help Dorian." Logan peered at him. "Just so he knows more about his classmates."

"That's difficult." The headmaster frowned. "I'd need a fully detailed academic agenda, which you haven't learned how to make yet. You can try, but I doubt you'll make a qualifying one before school starts." He reached for the door to the lobby.

"Headmaster?" I stopped him. "Can Logan come out into town tonight? It's for a friend's event."

The headmaster's shoulders drooped. He answered my question but addressed it to Logan instead of me.

"I'd advise against your leaving campus until further notice, Mr. Pierce." He shook his head. "I'm sorry if that means you miss out socially, but you'll be safest here."

"I trust your judgment, sir." Logan bent his head, letting Doris rub cheeks with him.

Just like that, Headmaster Hawkins let go of the doorknob and vanished.

"Maybe we can record Dylan's performance for you," I offered.

"Nah, it's Essex Street." Logan shrugged. "See you, Aliyah."

I didn't leave campus until the lobby door closed behind Logan. The entire walk home was spent hoping his situation might improve. Maybe I should have prayed instead.

CHAPTER ELEVEN

Open Mind Night
Dylan

On any other day, I loved the aroma of coffee and cookies—weird for a kid raised on tea and biscuits. But it was night, the kind with microphones at the Witch's Brew.

They'd packed the place to the rafters. Instead of five or six patrons rattling around like the last handful of peas in the tin, at least thirty people milled about.

I never minded being the center of attention. That was why I'd thought writing a spoken word piece and setting it against the backdrop of every power chord I could muster was a good idea. But the prose that came out wasn't my usual fare. Nothing humorous or even eye-rollingly corny visited my mind. Emo was more like it. Ugh.

Apparently, music magic was a thing. I couldn't use it, but once I saw the sizeable crowd, I thought maybe I should've tried learning it anyway. I hadn't bothered doing the research, and I'd called myself an overachiever back in London. So much for local coffee shop stardom. I'd flop, I knew it. Nothing felt more sure at that point in my life, less than a week after Grace Dubois had dumped me outside the Engine House, then sat there with our friends like the world hadn't ended.

There'd been no way to argue with her. I wanted to be with her, and I cared about her more than anyone I'd been with. She wanted to take things to the next level, and I'd kept her waiting on that for over six months.

Something about the idea of sex with Grace didn't feel right. Mum always said that when Dad kissed her, the world went away. Nothing close to that ever happened when Grace kissed me. I told her I just wasn't ready, but the truth was, I might never be, and I didn't know why.

I'd avoided everyone since then except for Lee Young. He was the chillest person at Hawthorn, so it was nearly impossible to feel awkward around him. He'd never been particularly good friends with Grace either, unlike the rest of my school chums.

I glanced down at the sign-up sheet. Fortunately, two people had signed up before me, so I wouldn't have to open, at least. I wouldn't have to perform at all if I didn't want to. I still hadn't taken the essential leap—inking my name on the paper. Without that last action, I'd be off the hook.

I almost walked away. None of the locals or tourists in this place cared if this particular air magus got on the stage. I wasn't famous, though some of my regular customers from Walgreens nodded and smiled in greeting.

That was it, then. I set the pen down and almost let it go. Maybe I could practice for another week. Perhaps I'd even manage to write a piece with at least one pun for the following Sunday. Nobody would know or care, I thought. I was wrong.

Gale, my dragonet, snored on the coat rack. Maybe he had the right idea—sleep this impulse and my misery off. But before the pen contacted the table's surface, I glanced up. Big mistake. I couldn't walk away since most of my friends had shown up.

Lee Young held the door open and Aliyah Morgenstern walked through it, leading the usual crew. She hadn't just brought Izzy and Cadence, either. Oh, no, practically everyone followed her in, kids from town and Hawthorn Academy and one I didn't recognize, a goth guy only slightly taller than Hal Hawkins.

There was one blessed absence from the usual crew, however. Grace Dubois was nowhere to be seen. If I'd spotted her, I would have done my best to look invisible and beat feet out the back door. I'd rather get up in front of Parliament in my skivvies than perform in a coffee shop with her in the audience.

Don't get me wrong. There's nothing horrible about Grace. It wasn't her fault my heart was broken. But the last thing I wanted was for her to hear these words I'd written about her. Her absence gave me strength.

I twirled the pen in my fingers, pointed the business end of it at the paper, and wrote my name on the third line. After that, I took a deep breath and carried my guitar over to the ordering line. A nice cold drink was a requirement at that point.

In the UK, I would've snuck a flask of whisky from Dad's study. But crossing the ocean was impossible, so I settled for red zinger tea on ice, extra honey. As I waited in line, something tugged at my elbow.

I looked down to find Ember, Aliyah's familiar, clutching my sleeve and peeping up a storm. She peered at the area around my neck and even tried looking down my shirt. Clearly, she hoped to see Gale. Our familiars were all friends, too.

"Peep?" She tapped my nose with her snout, then pulled her head back, blinking.

"He's over there, Ember." I jerked my chin at the coat rack beside the stained glass clock.

"Peep!" Ember took off, sweeping up toward the perch to meet her friend. He woke instantly and they jumped up and down, greeting each other and waving their tails. If only I was that happy to see my friends, but their presence only made me more nervous than I'd expected.

When the barista handed me my tea, I took it in a trembling hand but remembered to tip. I'd worked food service long enough to appreciate how much work she'd done. The glass was slippery and I worried about dropping it, even though I was one of the best athletes at school. I'd never been clumsy—an asset, I guess, with all the jobs I needed just to afford Hawthorn Academy.

I had a scholarship for tuition, but supplies and the mundane aspects of living were more expensive than most kids my age understood. You needed personal care items and clothes, basic stuff almost all of my classmates took for granted. That brought me back to why I'd ended up in a relationship with Grace: she knew that struggle firsthand. I closed my eyes, wishing I was back in my dorm practicing. At least that had felt something like solace.

Making a spectacle out of myself wasn't an issue until my feelings got involved. Not just feelings. I'd had those all my life and expressed them, but up until this summer, they'd been overwhelmingly positive. What bothered me was expressing the other side. I thought nobody would tolerate negativity. The things you learn in school, right?

"You mind if I come do this with you next week?"

I turned, finding the unfamiliar Hawthorn student behind me. As it turned out, he was slightly more punk than goth, though almost equal parts of both. A familiar perched on his shoulder, a white gryphon with the head of some sort of seabird.

"For open mic? No, I don't mind." I shrugged. "But I don't know why you'd need me around."

"Because if I'm not a complete idiot, you're Logan Pierce's roommate from Hawthorn Academy. I'm Dorian Spanos, your new classmate." He held out his hand. The gryphon tilted its head, cawing softly. "And this is Mercy."

"Dylan Khan. My familiar is Gale, the blue guy on the coat rack." I went to shake his hand, but he pulled back quickly.

"Too slow." Dorian grinned. "Seriously, man, thanks. Your roommate talked about you for like an hour today. He thinks you rock harder than diamonds."

"Logan?" I blinked. "He's here?"

"No, he had to stay on campus, but he asked me to say hi. He's mentoring me because I transferred from the Academy." Dorian snorted. "Lucky me, I get to start school on probation."

"Isn't that a task for the best student in the class?" I was surprised because my roommate couldn't have the top grades. He had a learning disability. More than one, with accommodations and everything. "Logan's—"

"Yeah, I know, right?" Dorian threw back his head and laughed. "Definitely doesn't seem like the brand of straight-laced on most eggheads, but there you go."

"Okay." I wasn't sure what Dorian meant by that. Logan took practically everything seriously. Had he changed? I didn't want to know, at least not during a bout of stage fright. "You're a poet, then?"

"Oh, no way." Dorian glanced at the barista waving at him. "You'll see sometime. Later, dude, my order's up."

"Later."

I scanned the room for an empty seat, someplace I could take a load off while waiting for my turn at the mic, but I saw nothing nearby. The only empty tables were over by the entrance, and I didn't want to walk all that way once they called me. Fortunately, there was a counter with plain wooden stools where I could set my drink down and lean for a while, so I took that option.

"Heard you were coming." I turned, finding Aliyah's brother Noah behind me. "Overheard a couple of other things too. Sorry about Grace."

"Oh, thanks, Noah," I said and nodded. "I didn't expect to see you at open mic night."

"I'm usually here in the summer. Just not last week." He glanced at my glass of tea, where my hand gripped it. "Nervous? It's okay if you are. Elanor gets butterflies every single time she sees the light that means they're recording. Calls it red-light fever, and she's been in front of a camera since birth, practically."

"I'm not usually nervous. It's just that tonight, the piece I'm doing is personal." I glanced at the crowd. "I thought it'd be totally dead in here."

"Well, that's the way the cookie crumbles." Noah elbowed my arm. "At least you've got a whole table of people rooting for you."

"Why don't you go sit with them?"

"They're all Aliyah's friends. And yours. Not mine."

"I'd like to think we all could get along."

"That's easier said than done in my experience." Noah turned his hand, curling his fingers to study his nails. "Things get complicated, especially when certain relationships end."

I didn't have much to say to that. Not anything I wanted to hear come out of my mouth, anyway, so I nodded. Even if I only partially agreed with Noah, his feelings were valid. He'd been through a bad breakup too.

The first act went on, a guy who introduced himself as Ethan. It was the telekinetic psychic who worked at the Engine House. He waited tables and ran the register there, using his powers to aid in his work. At times I envied him.

Levitating food and beverages to customers would have made my food service job on campus so much easier. But we are what we are, and I was an air magus, not a telekinetic psychic. Maybe someday I'd have enough control of my element to create that effect.

Ethan had music playing during his act but didn't utter a sound the entire time. His whole performance was telekinetic, done while standing almost perfectly still. He turned himself into something like the eye of a storm using various stuff from a bag he had on stage with him plus random things patrons brought up. They stepped forward one at a time, adding to the whirling collection around him.

The items from his bag all gave off light somehow. Some of them were glow sticks, the kind kids carried on Halloween while trick or treating. Others were flashlights, which he flipped on their axes to make strobing patterns. Napkins, stirrers, lids, and even cups joined them. He made patterns with the items, moving them back and forth around over and under each other. When he finished, he set every-thing down simultaneously in a semi-circle behind him on the small platform that served as a stage.

I was glad I wasn't second. I pulled the sheet of paper with my poem on it out of my pocket, glancing down at it. I felt like maybe it wouldn't be enough. Ethan's would be a hard act to follow.

The next performer didn't seem to mind, though. She looked

familiar in a vague way, like she was related to someone I knew. Her hair was reddish-orange and riotously curly like the Disney princess who accidentally turned her mother into a bear, but this woman was decades past thirteen. She wore a green t-shirt that said Redheads Have More Fun and carried a block of clay with her.

I blinked, shaking my head, wondering what kind of performance she could possibly do with that grayish cube of earth.

"That's Wanda Ambersmith, Azrael's cousin. She's a sculptor." Noah jerked his chin at the clay.

"That's not performance art." I blinked.

"Just watch her." His smirk was like a dare.

Noah was right. Without using her hands, Wanda shaped the clay before our eyes in a process reminiscent of time-lapse photography. She worked faster than any mundane sculptor I'd heard of, and more neatly too. In Creatives at school, some of us worked clay, but nobody in my year was an earth magus like Wanda. Time wasn't the only thing she didn't waste. All the clay became something, no excess cut off or moved aside.

At the end of her performance, she lifted a small statue off the table in front of her, holding it up for the entire crowd to see. My heart sank more spectacularly than the *Titanic* because it was a moon hare—Grace's moon hare, Lune. It even had the scar on his flank. My ex must've spent all her time with the Ambersmiths that summer. Must still be spending time with them.

Instead of the usual rounds of applause, spectators came up to have a look at the sculpture. That gave me time to run away. I grabbed at the paper with my poem, but it wasn't on the counter anymore. I glared at Noah, who held it up, lips moving as he read the words silently.

"I'm getting out of here," I snarled. "Give that back."

"You'll do no such thing." Noah held the paper over his head. "Your poem's amazing and needs to be spoken aloud. It's a little raw but totally moving. I understand why you don't want to do it here, not with this crowd, but you will get up there and play. I'll read this so you don't have to. Lord knows it's no foreign sentiment to me."

"What?" I blinked.

"Open your ears and your mind." Noah held the paper between us. "You heard me. I'll let you go if you're really not okay with this, but you'll owe me a favor later."

"No." I looked Noah in the eye, surprised at finding an unexpected ally, one who'd been through something quite similar the year before. "No need for that. Yeah, you can read it. And if anyone asks who wrote it, we don't answer."

"You're an odd duck, Dylan Khan, but not from a bad egg." Noah grinned when the MC called my name. "Let's go."

Noah sauntered toward the platform, stepping on top without breaking his stride. I followed, staying behind him. I used to play MMOs, the kind of video game where you team up with your mates and slay Internet dragons. In those teams, one player got in front of the others, took all the hits, and kept the boss occupied while the rest of the team laid out heaping piles of damage. We called them "The Tank."

Even though this open mic idea was all mine and I'd written the words, Noah Morgerstern stepped into the spotlight for me. He tanked that behemoth of a crowd, keeping their attention. If it wasn't for his decision to help, all the misery racing through my subconscious would have stayed under the surface, festering.

He waited until I'd strummed a few bars of the cobbled-together chords before speaking my words.

"An Open Mind

You said we'd always be open.
Arms, hearts, minds.
But I can't find
Any good reason
In this smolder season
Why I'm left behind.

All the things you were

And I wasn't.
What mattered to you but
Doesn't
Sit on my shoulders
Well, we're older
So smolder away
And away from me

Not close, you said, but
Closed like an airless
Space station
Separatist nation
Glottal vibration
I got tossed
So get lost
In someone new

Does it matter to you
How I can't breathe
Friends smile, try being cool
While I see the
Heartbroken
Unspoken word

I could find
An open mind
On every street corner.

And that might be what I need.
It's not what I want.

An open heart's more my speed."

Instead of just applause, cheers, whistles, and even a few howls sounded from all over the room. I'd only expected a response from my friends. Maybe Noah was right; maybe I had a talent besides manual labor and Bishop's Row.

But if so, I'd keep it on the down-low for the time being. Nobody had to know that poem was mine. Insisting on reading my words up there was Noah's way of telling me I wasn't alone. The territory I stood at the edge of was more well-traveled than expected, and someone who had no particular bias in my favor considered my feelings valid.

That made all the difference.

CHAPTER TWELVE

Aliyah

Noah went to Hawthorn Academy on his own the Sunday before classes started. He didn't even want Mom and Dad walking with him. I'm not sure what he was up to, but I definitely cared. He'd been quieter than usual since the open mic night. If that poem had anything to do with the state of his heart, I felt for him.

I had a sneaking suspicion that poem wasn't Noah's, even if it sounded like familiar fare from him. It could have been Dylan's. I wondered why neither of them claimed the credit. Had they collaborated? I tried asking Cadence and Izzy what they thought.

Cadence just shook her head, saying she felt bad for both of them. Izzy had nothing but disdain for the subject matter.

"Of all the things to write about, honestly. Romance." She snorted. "Dreadful way to ruin amazing friendships."

I'd left it at that. Izzy might never care much about romantic love, and that was okay, even if her opinion differed quite a bit from mine. As far as Cadence was concerned, Izzy's ideas could have come from another planet.

"It's okay if you don't believe in love, Iz." Cadence sighed. "I believe in it enough for both of us."

Izzy harrumphed and turned her back. The two of them said nothing more about the subject. I hoped they could keep from arguing about it while I was at Hawthorn. Izzy clung to opinions like a sloth to a tree and Cadence quoted everyone, from characters in books and movies to real-life people. The last thing I wanted was to come home from school one random weekend to find they'd stopped speaking to each other.

In any event, I wouldn't have walked straight over to Hawthorn. I'd promised Grace I'd meet her in front of the Ambersmiths' dress shop on Washington Street. She said she needed help with her things, and since I'd brought most of mine to campus the day Dorian arrived, I had plenty of hands.

"Wow, Grace!" I stopped on the curb and blinked at my roommate. "You look amazing."

"Thanks!" Her smile reminded me of a crescent moon. "I made this myself, and a whole wardrobe worth of other stuff." She gestured at the pile of garment and duffel bags on the sidewalk beside her.

This was the only time I'd seen Grace wear anything with a skirt outside of the formal dances last year. They looked good on her in general, but the one she had on now was particularly flattering. It had pleats and navy-blue piping that matched the school blazer perfectly. If that wasn't enough, the fabric she'd fashioned it from had a color-changing effect.

It wasn't iridescent, or anything like the mood rings Mom and Dad laughed about in the touristy trinket shops on Essex Street. In a way, it reminded me of the hypercolored shirts Bubbe showed me in pictures of Dad when he was my age, but the fabric on Grace's skirt wasn't anything so mundane. I could tell she'd used Umbral magic and something else mixed together on the fabric. It moved when she did, apparently activated kinetically.

"What did you do to that?"

"My own magic mostly, with a little changeling glamour. Azrael spent a couple of weeks in the dress shop with me, but his cousin told him to get lost after that. Fortunately, we worked on enough fabric together to make an entire wardrobe like this in my size."

Grace pulled aside her blazer to show me the shirt she'd paired with her outfit. Instead of the threadbare and utilitarian flannels of last year, her blouse rivaled the ones in designer shops on Newbury Street in Boston, and once again, this was a magical garment. It fit her like it had been sewn on, with no hint of mundane fasteners like buttons, zippers, or ties.

"You're going to be the best-dressed student this year." I hefted a bag, slinging it over my shoulder.

"Then my plan for school domination will go off without a hitch." Grace winked. "Somebody's got to give Temperance Fairbanks a run for her money. I've got plans, but first impressions matter, so clothes are important."

"Why you, though? I mean, it sounds like a lot of work and not much fun."

"Faith shouldn't have to deal with any more sibling rivalry. She deserves to just be contented with Hal all year." Grace sighed.

"Sounds like a good idea." I nodded, slinging on another bag to balance the weight. Hal's illness was terminal, so I agreed. He and Faith shouldn't have to waste any of their time together.

"Thank goodness I overheard Alex and Charity last year with you." Grace arranged the rest of her luggage on and across her body. "Their plan was to rule the school and sway public opinion against all the other extrahumans. I'm going to stop them, no matter what it takes."

"Can I help?"

"I'm not sure with what just yet, but definitely." Grace nodded. "Probably, you'll spend a lot of time looking otherworldly and vaguely threatening. Easy for you."

"I'm not sure any of us can really out-mean the mean girl, though."

"Yeah, nope. I'm going to out-cool the mean girl, then use niceness to get her into orbit." Grace snorted. "I'm Canadian, remember?"

We laughed our way across the street and around the corner to turn down Essex. Once there, we looked from side to side, searching for the magical migrating door. We found it next door to the Witch's Brew. As I reached to pull it open, Grace stopped me.

"I want a coffee before heading in there." Grace sighed, gazing down at her shoes. "I'd go to the café on campus, but that'll be awkward."

"Okay." I changed direction, heading into the coffee shop instead. We got in line, where I shuffled my feet before asking the million-dollar question.

"Hey, did you want to talk? About you and Dylan, I mean."

"There's not too much to talk about, at least not stuff I want to say in a crowded coffee shop. But things were kind of weird between us for a while."

It was our turn, so we ordered our drinks. Nothing fancy for me, just coffee with a splash of soymilk. Grace went all out and got a chocolate cherry mocha with extra whipped cream.

"You think he'll be okay?" I sprinkled cinnamon in my coffee.

"I'm not sure." Grace stuck a straw through the whipped cream. "I feel bad, but we didn't want the same things from each other. It's all private stuff."

We took our coffees and headed back out again. This time we marched straight through the door into the vestibule, then into the lobby at Hawthorn Academy.

Last year when I arrived, everything was strange, exciting, and far more awkward than expected. This year was totally different, thanks to Kitty, who'd arrived with her family shortly before us.

"Mama, Mom!" Kitty jumped up and down, squealing. "These are the friends I told you about, Grace and Aliyah. Girls, this is Mama, and that's Mom."

The trio of women smiled and waved. Kitty looked almost exactly like her mama, who was pale with ruddy hair and freckles. Her mom had curly dark hair, bronze skin, and a pair of golden wire-rimmed spectacles perched on her nose.

"It's so good to meet you." I held out a hand toward the women. "I got one of your makeup kits for Hanukkah last year, and it's been awesome."

"I'm so glad to hear that." Mom shook my hand. "And you were worried." She dropped a wink at Kitty's mama.

"Not anymore." Mama smiled.

"You came an awful long way to drop Kitty off at school." Grace grinned.

"It's on the way, actually." Mom adjusted her glasses. "We've got a health and beauty convention to attend in Boston later this week."

"Cool." Grace nodded.

"If you don't mind my asking, who's your designer?" Mama gave Grace's outfit an appraising glance. "Obviously, the blazer is the school's, but the rest of your ensemble is quite remarkable."

"I made them myself." Grace slipped her blazer off and turned in a slow circle, showing off her handiwork. "I spent the summer in an internship at Ambersmith Fashions, and this is what I did with my spare time."

"This is interesting. We've heard of Ambersmith, but many of their designs seem geared toward an older clientele."

"That's one reason I wanted to work with them." Grace nodded. "They could use a fresh perspective, I thought."

"Well, it's clear you're doing amazing things, Grace."

"Thanks so much. I appreciate it." Grace's cheeks reddened and she bowed her head, reminding me of the day she'd made first defense on the Bishop's Row team last year.

"Hey, Grace, Aliyah." Logan waved from the stairs. I watched him descend, with Dorian following.

Kitty's parents made their goodbyes and headed toward the door, while Kitty dragged her luggage toward the staircase, heading up after Logan and Dorian stepped off. I saw that while Logan wore a simple t-shirt and jeans with his blazer, Dorian's outfit would have looked at home in a Shrine of Hollywood catalog. Grace didn't match his goth theme, but the quality and care he'd put into his attire were on par with hers.

"Who's this, then?" Grace put on an enormous smile.

"This is Dorian Spanos from Rhode Island." Logan put on the good old Pierce family manners. "Dorian, this is Grace Dubois."

"Right, Aliyah's roommate." Dori took the hand she offered and shook it firmly. "The one who loves K-Pop, right?"

"Well, you're an enormous improvement over Alex Onassis." Grace wrinkled her nose. "Actually, that's not as nice as it sounded. Anything's an improvement over Alex."

"What's wrong with him?" Dorian raised an eyebrow.

"He's literally toxic. Poison magus, used to date my roommate. He flunked finals last year, so he's been held back. You're taking his spot."

"Oh, yeah, the bigot." Dorian nodded. "Logan told me a few things about that guy."

"Really?" I glanced at Logan.

"Only a little, I swear." Logan winced. "I figured somebody had to warn him."

"I'll catch him up the rest of the way." Grace snagged Dorian's arm, lacing hers through the crook of his elbow. "Let's have lunch. I bet we'll have loads to talk about."

As Grace escorted Dorian to the cafeteria, Logan and I stood there blinking. He scratched his head, and I shrugged.

"What just happened there?" I tilted my head.

"I'm not sure." Logan shook his head. "Dating's confusing."

"I cornered the market on that," I said, smiling. "I guess maybe you did too."

"I might be imagining this, but I think Grace grew up an awful lot over the summer."

"No, I agree with you. This new Grace has got a purpose, too."

I sauntered toward the café with Logan, filling him in about my roommate's plans. We stopped at the end of the line, where upperclassmen stood waiting to order coffee from none other than Dylan Khan. One of them turned, revealing a familiar face.

"I'm not judging, Aliyah, but aren't you caffeinating a bit too much?"

"No, Darren, I'm good." Noah still avoided his ex-boyfriend, but he wasn't my enemy. "Just waiting with Logan. He could use a latte or three, don't you think?"

"Perhaps." Darren nodded. "He's been working hard."

"Yeah, Dorian's a handful," Logan replied. "He's had me running around with him all over campus this past week."

"If you ask me, it's that gryphon of his." Darren jerked his chin at Dorian's familiar, who'd perched on the edge of the garbage can between the café and the cafeteria. "That critter seems to be all over the place."

"That's pretty typical of the species." I shrugged. "My grandma says she requires a security deposit for boarding them. What can you do?"

"Make sure he's in Familiar Bonding for one thing." Logan sighed. "Looks like I'll be back there again this year if only to help Dorian through it. I think his familiar needs it more."

"Maybe I'll go too." I grinned. "Second-years on probation can opt-in."

"You hardly need that. I mean, look at the two of you." Darren nodded at Ember, who'd been sleeping on my shoulder half the morning. "Thicker than thieves."

"Maybe I want to keep my friend company and meet some new people." I sighed. "Also, I'm still on probation. Any good deed will help me in that department."

"If you ask me, they came down too hard with your punishment." Darren turned toward the counter and ordered a pot of tea from Kayleigh, the café's manager. She beckoned him toward the other end of the counter. "Anyway, I'm sure I'll see you two around the lounge."

"See you later, Darren." I waved.

We finally got to the counter, where Dylan stared at the doorway to the cafeteria. On weekdays, it was closed, but on weekends and during school breaks, it was open. It perfectly framed Grace sitting with Dorian, the two of them laughing at a booth over sandwiches and beverage roulette.

"You okay, man?" Logan leaned on the counter.

"I'll deal." Dylan's voice sounded unusually flat. I didn't like it. "What are you ordering?

"Nothing, just saying hi." Logan blinked.

"Well, hi. There's a line behind you. They kind of pay me to help them, and once I'm through this one, I'm off-shift."

"No, wait," I added. "Get Logan a triple latte. I think he needs it." I jerked a thumb at Logan's puffy eyes.

"Okay." Dylan busied himself with the espresso machine, pouring the shots into a cup and adding frothed milk. "Here you go."

"Dylan, do you want to hang out at the welcome party?"

"Maybe, but I'm leaving at the first possible minute. Totally worn out. You don't want me around. I'm a stick-in-the-mud lately."

I blinked, unsure what to say to that, but luckily, Logan had an answer.

"That's okay, I don't want to watch Elanor parade around either. After they introduce the first-years, I'm out too."

"Thanks, bro." The tension in Dylan's shoulders eased. "I'll appreciate the company. Next!"

We got out of the way so Dylan could finish helping the line. I knew his manager would get back to the counter soon, but for now, we had to let him do his job.

"What's next for you, Aliyah?"

"I guess I'm taking Grace's luggage upstairs." I pointed at the suitcase and bag she'd left sitting beside the staircase, then at the ones I still carried.

"I'll help."

He grabbed some luggage with me and we stepped on the first stair, calling out the third floor. Once we got to my room, Logan left the cases, saying he'd better check on Dorian.

If Grace was enlisting him in her quest for cool, Logan and I might end up doing a lot of behind-the-scenes work for them. Maybe I'd like to be in the background for a change. During last year's first two days at Hawthorn Academy, I had been the center of disaster and unwanted attention.

As it turned out, I was wrong about all of that.

"We just didn't want the same things from a relationship, Aliyah." Grace held a blouse with mother-of-pearl buttons between her and the mirror. "He's amazing, smart, funny, and athletic, but what can you do?"

"Not break up?" I slipped one of my spare school blazers on a hanger. "I don't understand, maybe because I didn't even really like Alex. But what do you mean, the same things?"

"Oh." Grace's face in the mirror reddened. "Aliyah, I'm talking about sex."

"Like, he pressured you?" I blinked, unable to imagine Dylan Khan leering and looming like boys in movies.

"Yeah, no." Grace shook her head. "More like the other way around."

"Um." My fingers fumbled, the tunic I held dropping back into the suitcase.

"I stopped, of course." Grace sighed. "He wasn't comfortable, I could tell. The first time was that night you walked in on us. I asked him if he was ready and he said no but that he loved me, so I waited. Over the summer, I asked again. Same thing. I realized it just wouldn't work."

"Oh, Grace. I'm sorry."

You're not and you know it. March out of here this instant and ask that boy on a date. See what happens.

"No." Grace said it, not me. My jaw dropped because for a moment, I thought she'd heard the Evil Inside Voice. "There's nothing to be sorry about. Some people just aren't compatible, no matter how much they care about each other."

"Are you okay?"

"I'll live." Grace snorted. "I've got outfits to rock, mean girls to outdo. Having something to keep me busy helps. And that you're not walking on eggshells around me."

"What do you mean?"

"Logan's giving me the cold shoulder." She sighed. "Can't blame him after I dumped his roommate."

"I'm not sure that's just about Dylan, though."

"What do you mean?"

"His life's a mess," I said, and I told her all about the last couple of weeks.

"Leaping Luna." Grace whistled. "I understand now why the headmaster's confining him to campus, but it sucks. What's he going to do on Parents' Night? They showed up last time."

"I don't know." I moved to the dresser with a stack of leggings. "I haven't asked him yet."

"There's time, I guess." Grace put the rest of her clothes away in the wardrobe, then opened another bag and started stowing pairs of shoes under her bed. They all looked new.

"Did you make those over the summer, too?" Last year, she'd only had one pair of sneakers.

"No, Az did. He ended up doing a good job at his uncle's shop. Definitely cobbler material, that guy."

"That's a pretty significant gift, Grace."

"Not really." She shrugged. "I'm the one who convinced his uncle to give him a chance there. At least, that was what Azrael said when he gave these to me."

"Well, he's always been a good kid."

"Izzy disagrees." Grace raised an eyebrow. "Says he's obsessive. I didn't get that impression."

"She's hands-off in the displays of affection department. Really, they're different from each other." I glanced down at the row of shoes. "We all are. That's what you were saying earlier, right?"

"Yeah, Aliyah." Grace stood, holding her arms out. "And sometimes, exactly the same."

We hugged, then left the rest of our unpacking for later so we'd make the welcome assembly on time.

CHAPTER THIRTEEN

I sat in the front row again like last September. Other repeats included Headmaster Hawkins appearing out of nowhere and Grace sitting with me, but this time, the rest of our year joined us. We took up all the seats in front of the podium, baffling the students in Noah's year, who stuck to the back.

"Stealing the scene. I like it." Hal peered around Faith and me, grinning at Grace.

"Good." Faith clutched his hand and nodded at me. "Because here comes trouble."

Grace stared placidly ahead at the headmaster, posture straight enough to balance a stack of books on her head. She'd said earlier that I was supposed to look otherworldly and vaguely threatening, so that's what I kept in mind when I turned to see what Faith meant. Or rather who.

Even without my ex escorting her, I would have recognized the girl walking across the room as Temperance Fairbanks. For one thing, she was built along the same lines as her sisters, despite her darker hair. For another, hard laughter dropped from her lips like diamonds into a lead-crystal vase.

I narrowed my eyes, nostrils flaring. Ember stood up on my shoulder, wings out and hissing softly.

Good, you sense that power, then. She's got more than the other two. Possibly even you.

"What's her element?" I murmured to Faith.

"Water," she whispered back.

I considered the implications. The other water magi I knew were deep, a bit quiet, and generally pleasant people. In our studies last year, Professor Luciano had taught that water was a sympathetic element, able to comprehend and conform temporarily while retaining its essential nature. Logan exemplified that, so how could Temperance Fairbanks be as horrible as Faith implied?

Because she understands of course, foolish girl.

That made no sense, so I tuned the Evil Inside Voice out and watched Alex bow slightly while waving her toward a seat in the center aisle across from Grace and one row back. They sat right behind Kitty and Eston, whom Alex greeted despite the chilly reception Kitty gave him. Eston stared at his shoes, mumbling something about a long drive.

"It's not like you think." Faith murmured. "Her water magic, I mean."

I'd ask her what that meant later because Headmaster Hawkins took that moment to begin his speech.

"Welcome, students." This year, Headmaster Hawkins didn't smile, and I couldn't fault him for it. His son sat in the same row with me, after all, and he looked ashy and thinner than he should have. Hal hadn't even had a growth spurt.

"Summer is over, and it's time to settle in for the new school year. Since brevity served me well last year, I'd like to rely on it again. However, that's not in the cards this time."

Ah, yes, the chaos to come.

I sighed and tried to tune out the Evil Inside Voice. The assembly information had to be important.

"Your rooming assignments come from the pneumatic tubes to my left. Your class schedules should already be in your rooms; check the desks. First Years will report back here for their campus tour after lunch." Headmaster Hawkins cleared his throat. "I want every student to make as much effort as possible to get into the routine this first month because in October, extramurals will begin."

"You'll be hosts and ambassadors to students from Gallows Hill School and Wolf Messing Preparatory. I expect you to treat them with care and respect, as you'd wish to be treated if they hosted us on their campuses. Even though we'll be competing in many events against our guests, some projects will require your collaboration with a diverse group of extrahuman peers and their teachers."

Like last year, Headmaster Hawkins stopped his speech to make eye contact with each student in the room. When our eyes met, I felt a sense of welcome, which eased the tension in my shoulders. Even Ember settled down, but that feeling was short-lived. As his gaze shifted to the next row, I watched his knuckles pale as he gripped the sides of the podium tighter. His Adam's apple bobbed as he swallowed nothing.

I looked over my shoulder. He'd locked gazes with Temperance, and from the way her eyes narrowed and his widened, he didn't like what he'd seen. He moved along to the next student but took less time with each of them than last year.

"You see?" Faith whispered.

"Yeah." I nodded.

"You're all dismissed. The welcoming party will commence in this very room after dinner this evening."

Students rose from their seats or leaned forward, chatting with each other. Our group did the same. Grace and Dorian stood at the head of the room, smiling brightly even though their words to us were anything but.

"Read any good essays this summer, Hal?" Grace asked, raising her eyebrow.

"No." Hal sighed. "I mean, I read some, but most weren't good."

"Give us the bad news first." Dorian tilted his head.

"Sorry about your sister, Dorian."

"Oh." He shook his head, cheeks red. "Well, that's not the bad news I meant."

"You did it again, Hal." Grace sighed, shaking her head.

"Give him a break, he's due at the infirmary in a half-hour." Faith stood up.

"Why not talk about this there?" I offered. "Hal won't be late for Nurse Smith, and it's bound to be more private than the lobby."

Nobody said anything, but most of my classmates clearly agreed. Grace, Dorian, Logan, Kitty, and Eston followed Hal and Faith toward the infirmary. I started to bring up the rear when Lee Young stopped me.

"What's up?"

"More like down and who." Lee tilted his head toward the other side of the lobby.

"Dylan." I nodded. "I'll go over and talk to him."

"Wait," Lee said. "I know you get distracted sometimes, but try and remember to keep an eye out for him. He's not doing so great, and everything I've tried isn't helping much."

"Then why are you asking me?" I blinked. "You're the one who notices this stuff. It's kind of like your superpower."

"You're kidding, right?" Lee blinked back.

"No."

"If my superpower is noticing, then yours is helping. Whatever you try, when it's for someone else, it works." He grinned, fist-bumping my shoulder. Before I could make any reply, he headed toward the stairs with Scratch bouncing behind him. That was how I ended up alone, staring across the room at the wall Dylan leaned against.

It was almost the same spot I'd stood in the year before, despairing about fitting in or even making it through the first week of school. Someone I cared about had gotten himself stuck in the same position, which nearly broke my heart.

You had it bad. Why shouldn't he suffer alone as you did?

"Why should he, when I could help?"

Indeed. So why are you standing around?

So, this particular bout of negativity in my heart and mind didn't come from the Evil Inside Voice. Instead, it was garden-variety self-doubt telling me Dylan Khan wouldn't want any sympathy from me. I almost turned my back on him, but someone wouldn't let me.

"Peep?" Ember craned her neck, twisting it until her eyes were level with mine. Then, she tapped me on the top of the head with her tail. "Peep. Peep!"

After that, she launched off my shoulder, sailing toward Dylan with the enthusiasm and speed she usually reserved for me. She left me little choice but to follow her. I wasn't sure what to say, so I just leaned against the wall beside him.

We stood in silence, neither daring to break it. Ember and Gale swooped back and forth in front of us. I turned my head to look at Dylan and saw that he stared straight ahead, watching the dragonets. Finally, he spoke.

"What's he like?"

"Hmm?"

"The new kid." Dylan swallowed. "The one she's spending so much time with."

"Oh." I turned, putting my right shoulder against the wall instead of my back so I could face my friend. "Dorian reminds me of Cadence, but not a girl, and monochrome instead of rainbow."

"Cadence is good, right? I mean, she wouldn't, um, hurt anyone?" The extra sheen over Dylan's eyes meant he needed an answer.

"Not on purpose, no." I shook my head, even though he wasn't looking at me. "I think they're just being friendly, for what it's worth."

"I'd say that's worth about pocket lint." Dylan closed his eyes. "You're clueless about that stuff, Aliyah."

"That's fair."

"And honestly, who wouldn't like Grace DuBois? She's awesome." All the air went out of him. His breath hitched as he took one to speak again. "Lee came up to the counter this morning. Talked at me about some kind of 'this too shall pass' stuff."

"He's not wrong." I sighed. "But getting through the time before stuff passes? That's harder than it should be."

"You don't really understand." He finally turned his head. The corners of his eyes held teardrops like cut glass. "I'm alone in this."

"Nah. Saw you with Noah at the Open Mic. He gets it."

"Yeah." Dylan's gaze softened. "He said I can talk to him any time, but I don't want to."

"So, what do you want?" After uttering those words, I could barely breathe. I didn't know why.

"To be with my friends and forget about her for a little while, but that feels impossible. They all went off with her like she's Miss Salem or something." The tear staining his cheek gave my voice back.

"I'm still here."

"Thanks for that, Aliyah." Dylan turned, mirroring my stance against his section of the wall. "So, can you tell me why?"

I blinked, unsure what he asked for until he continued.

"What's with the Fashion Week wardrobe? Why are they following her like a pack of coyotes? And why did she choose Dorian to hang all over?"

"Dorian's got the charisma to pull weight in a power couple. Because she's trying to rival Te—"

"And here we have the mad pyromaniac and the class clown." Alex's voice sounded far too close to my back.

"Funny," a sweet-toned feminine voice said. "But looks aren't everything."

I stood up straight and turned. This put my eyes almost on a level with Alex's, so I gave him my best glare. My anger kept my vision to a tight focus, so for the time being, I ignored the girl at his side.

"Poison the air someplace else, Onassis," I hissed.

Alex snorted. "Discriminate much?"

"Relax, Alexander." The feminine voice spoke again. "It's the lobby. Anyone can be here. And if Miss Disciplinary Probation Morgenstern makes trouble, I'll take it to the headmaster."

I turned to face the speaker, and the first thing I noticed was that her hair wasn't the same close up as it had seemed from afar. It reminded me of water in a creek, brown with deep undertones. She'd bleached out the underneath and dyed it dark green. I soon saw why.

A pair of tentacles the same hue slid along the right shoulder of the girl's blazer. A moment later, a head moved out from behind her neck, eyes shining at me from under her earlobe. I'd seen one of these before.

"Grundylow." I blinked, everything I'd read about them coming out of my mouth before I could stop it. "Spawn of Grendel, loves brackish water and drowning things. Associates with water magi."

"Told you she was a total nerd about critters." Alex rolled his eyes and tugged her sleeve. "You saw she-who-shall-not-be-named and one of her charity cases, Tempe. Let's go do something else."

"Wait, which is this one?" She flicked her pinkie at Dylan. "The orphan?"

"Nah." Alex shook his head. "He's the over-caffeinated clown."

"Could have fooled me." She shrugged and turned her back on us, linking her arm through Alex's and sauntering away.

As Temperance Fairbanks walked away, the grundylow parted her hair and stared at me. Its grin curved, matching the angle of the knobby horns on its head, which reminded me of the brambles that grow in seaside swamps.

"So, I guess we've met the new mean girl."

"Definitely not the same as the old one." I jerked my chin at the eerie critter. "We'll have to watch out."

We didn't know the half of it.

CHAPTER FOURTEEN

During the welcome party later that night, I acted as a shuttle between Dylan and the rest of our friends. I refused to abandon him, but I needed to back Grace up from time to time. Mostly, though, she had a good handle on her new circumstances. By that, I mean the altitude she'd gained in the popularity stratosphere.

Elanor Pierce stopped to chat with Grace more than once. Last year, Elanor didn't give the kids in our year the time of day. Temperance and Alex had a gaggle of new students hovering around them, but not for long. By the time the magipsychic slideshow showcasing the new first-years began, several of them had approached Grace and Dorian to see what all the fuss over them was about. Two even stuck around.

I needed a break from the constant churn of social activity and ended up leaning against the wall with Dylan to catch my breath. Ember perched on the chandelier with Gale.

"Looks like she's getting on." Dylan stared across the room, letting his eyes wander amongst the people in Grace's orbit.

"Check out her competition, Dylan." I jerked my thumb at the smaller throng of kids in the corner with Temperance Fairbanks. "If you can call it that."

"And we thought Charity knew what she was doing, sending Temperance to be the new It Girl." He snorted. "That stumble's worse than Logan out on the Bishop's Row court."

"Be nice." I elbowed Dylan's shoulder. "Nobody's good at everything, and he needs all the help he can get lately."

"It's just a basis for comparison. I didn't mean to insult my mate." Dylan sighed. "It seems like everything I do is all wrong."

"I get it."

"Yeah. Thanks for understanding, Aliyah." He waved his hand, dismissing the crowd. "Being here in the corner."

"There's no way I'd leave a friend all alone." I swallowed, praying I wouldn't blush.

"Right. Being nice, it's punk as fu—" Dylan put his hand over his mouth, eyes wide "I can't believe that almost slipped out, sorry."

"Awkwardness sort of compounds on itself, like interest on a bad loan." My face felt flushed, though he wasn't looking at me anymore. "But it gets better, Dylan."

"You're being summoned again." Dylan nodded toward the throng of people around our friends. This time it wasn't Grace beckoning me over but Hal Hawkins.

"Will you be okay for a few minutes?" I raised my eyebrow, awaiting his response.

Dylan gave me a grin rarer than diamonds. "Yeah, I'm okay."

I patted his shoulder before heading toward Hal. Ember swooped down, peeping over her shoulder at Gale as she perched on my shoulder. Crossing the room wasn't as difficult as it might have been for Hal with his energy-sapping illness. I stood behind him and Faith, whose arm he clung to.

"What's up?"

"As soon as they show the last student, I'm out. Let's bring Dylan with us." Hal took a few short, shallow breaths before continuing, "Faith's staying, but I need help navigating a room this packed."

"No problem." I glanced at Faith Fairbanks. "You sure you don't want to go with Hal and leave the socializing to me?"

"Oh, you can't always get what you want." She sighed. "I need to keep an eye on them." She jerked her chin at Temperance and Alex.

"All the more reason for us to switch tasks." I raised an eyebrow. "Or do you think I can't handle him like I did last year?"

"I know you can, but I'm the one who knows Tempe's tells. Anyway, you're a sledgehammer, and this is a scalpel job. I've got Alex covered; got a new preventive tactic."

"Okay?" I blinked. "Care to elaborate?"

"Meet me for a swim tomorrow night and we'll talk about it."

"Sure." I nodded. Faith and I hadn't worked together magically. Our skills weren't compatible, more like oil and water, but teamwork might be the key to surviving this year. However, something might throw a monkey wrench into our swimming plans.

"Don't we have to worry about Tempe invading the public bathroom?"

"She's on the second floor and lazy. There's no way she'd come all the way to the third floor to use ours."

"It's starting, look."

The magipsychic display lit up. A series of faces with familiars and names flashed across it, simultaneously announced over speakers in the chandeliers. The first was one I recognized, an Ambersmith, not a sibling of Azrael's but one of his cousins. Her name was Giselle, and she had a raven familiar, which didn't surprise me. I remembered her as insatiably curious and secretive, so a raven fit perfectly. She was one of the first-years hanging with Grace.

Next was Temperance, her grundylow grinning eerily at the screen. His eyes seemed to meet mine, making me shiver. A blond boy with a buzz cut followed her. He wore horn-rimmed glasses and held a cat familiar in his arms. His name escaped me.

My heart almost stopped when the next student showed up, partly because at first glance, his last name looked like Morgenstern. I blinked and shook my head and read Magnuson, Arick. He had the same initials, but the uncanny coincidences ended there. Arick had tousled shoulder-length light-brown hair with a pair of small plaits behind each ear, Nordic style. He stood near Dorian and had no familiar. I guess we'd see him in Familiar Bonding, then.

Alex Onassis flashed up on the screen. I turned away. If only I could ignore him for the entire school year. But that would be impossible. I needed to help my friends counter Temperance's machinations, and he was firmly and clearly on her team. We'd confront each other sooner or later. I might be the only person he feared on this campus.

I'd lost count of the number, but the next student I noted in the slideshow was the last one. Michelina Zanelli had brassy blonde hair and tanned olive skin. Like Arick, she had no familiar, but she stood alone behind the refreshment table like I had last year.

"And we're out." Hal rested a hand on my arm.

"I'll make sure he gets upstairs safely, Faith."

"Thanks."

I escorted Hal Hawkins across the room, locking eyes with Dylan as we got closer to his section of the wall, I felt Ember tug my hair, so I helped Hal lean against the wooden surface and turned.

"Hi." A boy stood behind me, extending his hand for a shake. "I'm—"

"Arick Magnuson, I saw." I nodded. "It's nice to meet you, but I'm kind of busy right now."

"I just wanted to ask how you got your dragonet." He glanced at Hal, his brow wrinkling. "Are you okay?"

"Hal's not feeling too well." I shook his hand. "Stop by my table at breakfast or dinner and we'll talk."

"Oh." When the handshake ended, he turned his hand palm up and stared at it like he'd just met a celebrity.

Oh, no. It seems you've got a fan club. Infamy is greater than fame.

Hal leaned more heavily on my arm, nearly throwing me off-balance.

"Come on, Hal, let's get you upstairs." Dylan came to support him on the other side. "See you later, Magnuson."

"Yeah, later."

We didn't speak again until I asked the stairs for the third floor.

The only sound on the way up was Dylan's yawn. Once we reached the top, Hal finally said something.

"You're someone's role model already." Hal grinned, lips pale and eyes sleepy. "Good going."

"Maybe." I shook my head. "But what could he know except that I'm an extramagus? The last person who considered that awesome was Alex."

"It's probably Ember." Dylan raised his eyebrow. "Dragonets attract loads of attention. I mean, I know from personal experience and everything."

"Thanks, Dylan." I sighed. "I hope you're right."

"It can't be that bad, surely?" Dylan shook his head. "I've never seen Alex go for someone who wasn't attractive. I mean, look at Darren."

Hal sighed. "I'm sure all his interest in her came from the extramagus thing. He must have asked me a hundred questions about her powers after Valentine's Day last year."

I felt like I'd been frozen in a block of ice because this wasn't something I expected other people to understand, let alone point out. I stopped walking in the middle of the hall.

"Thanks, Captain Obvious." Dylan blinked. "You broke Aliyah."

"Sorry." Hal's forehead wrinkled, making him look just like his father for a moment. "I didn't mean to upset you. I just don't feel like I have time to mince words."

"I knew all this, but I didn't expect anyone else to notice." I took a deep breath and continued on our way toward his room. "At least you unleashed that now instead of mid-crisis or something."

"Yeah." Dylan nodded. "As much as I'd like to laugh and say what crisis, I worry we'll have more than one this year."

As we waited for Hal to palm the plate next to his door and go inside, I realized Dylan was on to something. Fewmets would hit the fan eventually, probably several times once extramurals started. If I'd had a djinn's lamp, I would've wished for him to be wrong, but even magical wishes might not equalize the social battles ahead.

CHAPTER FIFTEEN

The first-day lecture should have felt like a review. Professor Luciano talked about a subject most extrahumans had been hearing about since early childhood: coincidence.

"The idea of fate is as old as humanity." As he spoke, an illustration of three women at a loom appeared on the chalkboard. "Extrahumans know more about it because of our connection with the Under, and by association, with changelings and their faerie parents. Destiny is not as simple as the idea that your path was decided before birth. It works in patterns, cycles that could be either followed or broken. We call that coincidence."

Luciano's take was extremely old-school, likely a product of his education at the oldest extrahuman universities in the world. Or perhaps because of his Italian citizenship and heritage. The cradle of magus society was the Mediterranean.

"As adult magi, you'll need to know how to recognize, research, and track coincidental patterns. Your third-year studies will largely focus on that. For now, I want you to begin paying attention. Anything that looks like a pattern should be noted and discussed with your peers during library time. At the end of the year, you'll turn in a brief personal essay about what you noticed."

Everyone furiously scribbled notes, even Logan, who always got a transcript of the lecture as part of his IEP accommodations. Everyone must have found this idea and the assignment interesting. It gave me a strange feeling, like part of my brain had floated up to the ceiling.

Maybe that's why I went through the motions for the rest of the day until Gym, which shook me out of the odd funk.

"Listen up, kiddos, because I'm only telling you once!" Coach Pickman clapped her hands to get our attention. "You might be second-years, but you're still twerps to me. If you want to make the extramural Bishop's Row team, you'll work your hinies off, starting this minute."

She stopped in front of Dorian, who stood with his hand in the air, a tactic that had worked wonders on Professor Luciano that morning. It flew about as adeptly as a waterlogged pigeon with Coach Pickman.

"Spanos. What's your problem?"

"I'm just checking. You got the note from Nurse Smith, right?"

"Necessary medical device, boo-fricking-hoo. You're still running laps. Everyone new to me does. I made Hawkins do it last year with his note, and you're no different."

"But, Coach!"

"No buts in my gym unless they're on the court running laps. Snap to it, Spanos!" She clapped her hands so close to his nose I thought she'd pinch it.

She turned her back on Dorian, which was a good thing under the circumstances. He dropped his jaw, then narrowed his eyes as he snapped it shut. The look my classmate gave the coach was like a hail of arrows on a battlefield. As I sauntered toward the starting line marked on the track around the court, I slowed my pace to walk beside Dorian.

"Dude, she's harsh but fair most of the time. It'll be okay. Just run the laps. Look at it this way; you can't be any slower than Logan. He's practically a turtle."

"Easy for you to say. He said you're the fastest kid in our year." Dorian hung his head, tugging on the section of shirt covering his chest. It clung oddly like he wore something under it. "This is going to hurt."

"I'm sorry. She's only tough at the beginning. If you have any problems today, she'll find something else for you to do."

"Maybe your psychic friend can give me a reading about gym class." Dorian rolled his eyes. "Thanks for checking on me, from one delinquent to another."

"Lee Young says giving a damn is my superpower." I shrugged. "Who am I to argue with that?"

Coach Pickman's whistle cut off our conversation. Like last year, the simplicity of running lulled me into a sense of calm, which was a tough state to attain at school. Gym was one of my only escapes from feeling like a misfit on this campus. If I were perfect, I'd love it here, but I'd learned last year that nobody was.

You could be, with a little work in the right direction.

"No." I disguised my response to the Evil Inside Voice in measured breathing as I paced my run. Last year, it had wanted me to give in to my temper and live up to my mother's notorious Hopewell heritage. Instead, I'd decided to do everything I could to stay good.

I glanced over my shoulder and saw Logan and Dorian at the back of the pack, though Dorian's face was red and he was sweating far more than I'd expected. Maybe he had mundane asthma or something. I hoped it wasn't an awful magical malady like Hal's.

Without Alex Onassis in our class this year, I pretty much had no competition on the track. Faith paced herself well and was the next fastest, but she still ate my dust. I hoped to get on the extramural team this year, but it was a long shot even with my speed.

Elanor Pierce was the star player at our school, and my brother Noah was a close second in ability and skill. In our year, Dylan and Grace were both better athletes than me. Lee and I would probably compete for the last slot on that team, with one of us on reserve. If we got that far. There were three other students in Noah's year who'd give us a run for our money.

I watched Hal press the button on the stopwatch as I passed the finish line, then I leaned forward with my hands on my knees, just breathing. When Faith pulled up after me, we both sat on the bench near him.

"Sorry, Aliyah." She shook her head. "I'm not much of a challenge in here."

"That's okay, I can take it easy for now. Lab's next, are you ready?"

"As long as Luciano doesn't start with the hardest experiment again, I am."

"I promise to put out any fires, whether I start them or not." I put my right hand on the left side of my chest.

"No more fires." Bailey, the next classmate to finish laps, managed those three words through her athletically-induced huffing and puffing.

"It wasn't my fault, Bailey."

"Not the second time." She rolled her eyes, then sighed. "Give your sob story to my sister."

"Hmmm?" I blinked. What in the world was Bailey talking about?

"I'm never switching to Team Dubois." She snorted.

"Whatever." Faith narrowed her eyes. "Why bother talking to us then, Bailey?"

"Hit the locker rooms, kiddos!" Coach Pickman jerked her thumb at the doorway.

"We're not trying on any gear?" Logan blinked.

"No." Coach Pickman crossed her arms over her chest shaking her head. "There's only two of you with any chance of making the team. Next time, we're focusing on mundane sports. Remedial, but hopefully fun. Catch my drift?"

"We're too early for Lab." Hal set the stopwatch aside, along with the notepad he'd used to record times. "What should we do?"

"Report back here after you're cleaned up and in your regular clothes. I've got something to show you."

We all headed to the locker room as she'd instructed, even Hal, who hadn't done anything besides change into his uniform. Our locker rooms had one common area with benches and hooks for bags and blazers, with sauna access, a steam room, and a first-aid station.

The middle doorway led to a smaller gender-neutral locker room, the one on the left was just girls and just boys on the right.

Even though it hadn't been a challenge, I'd exerted myself, so I went to the girl's side and rinsed off in the shower before changing. When I emerged, Dorian still sat in his gym uniform, ridiculous purple shorts and all. It looked like he was waiting for something, although everyone else was dressed and gathering their school blazers.

"You okay, Dorian?" I stopped and sat on the bench next to him.

"Yeah." He took a few deep ones. "I can change fast. Don't worry."

"It wasn't about changing, it's the health stuff. After that run, are you all right?"

"Yeah. Hal said you were one of the first to notice something was up with him. I get it, but I'm okay. It's physical, but I can deal."

"Okay." I nodded, standing up. "If you need anything, you know where to find me."

"You're the nicest miscreant I've ever met." Dorian chuckled. "And that's saying a lot. The Academy's full of them."

"Thanks, I guess. See you out there."

Dorian must've been the master of fast changes because, by the time I'd found a spot on the bleachers, he emerged from the locker room in his regular clothes. I gave him a quick smile as he walked across the court.

"Morgenstern, Fairbanks. You can goof off because I want you both at tryouts for Bishop's Row. The rest of you pay attention." Coach Pickman pointed her whistle at the ceiling. The scoreboard descended.

I should say it served as the scoreboard on every other occasion I'd seen it. This time, it looked like the screen out in the lobby, and there weren't any scores on it. Instead, it displayed a PowerPoint presentation.

I didn't goof off, but I didn't study the subject raptly either. I'd seen something like it before from Cadence. Coach Pickman was telling the class about cheer squads. She recited words off the slides in a monotone, giving the impression she'd had nothing to do with its creation.

"Coach Chen is organizing a cheer squad. If you have questions or want to join, talk to him." Coach Pickman put her whistle to her mouth and gave it three sharp blasts. "Dismissed!"

We filed out of the gym, entering the hallway in one group. The doors were wide enough to allow for that, and it let me get a look at Logan's face. His eyes were alight, like the day he'd met Doris. I hadn't seen him this excited for a long time.

"So, cheer squad, huh?" I smiled.

"Yeah, looks like it." He grinned. "I bet I'll see Kitty there, and Eston too."

"Maybe me if I don't make the team. Which seems likely."

"You'll make it." Dorian elbowed my shoulder. "Grace isn't going out for Bishop's Row this year."

"Oh?" I blinked.

"Yeah, says she wants to leave it for Dylan. He loves it, and it's not her favorite thing."

"I still have to worry about all the third-years, plus Faith, Lee, and my brother." I shrugged. "Not to mention that part of my probation came from an incident at Bishop's Row last year, so I might not even be eligible."

"You are." Hal held the door to magipsychic lab for Faith and stood there keeping it open for the rest of us. "My dad said he's letting everybody try out."

"Even Alex?" I raised an eyebrow.

"Yes."

"Bummer." Dorian snorted. "I can't stand that guy."

"You haven't even met him."

"I met Noah last night, who mentioned your ex a few times. His reputation precedes him."

"So does mine."

"Yours is like a patchwork quilt, while his is all one color." Dorian shook his head.

I shrugged. "Still, it's better to form your own opinion, don't you think?"

"Didn't he put a poison whammy on you?" Dorian blinked. "Why defend someone like that?"

"I don't know." I stared at my hands.

You do—first kiss and all. But you won't tell Mr. Spanos that.

"Maybe because I don't want to tell you what to think about someone else." I squared my shoulders, looking Dorian in the eye. "You can find out for yourself."

"Facts are facts, Miss Morgenstern." Professor Luciano did his usual butting in, which was his right in his classroom, after all. "The most salient fact at present is that Lab starts now, and you haven't chosen a bench or a partner."

He was right. I looked around the room, noticing that Hal and Faith sat together this time. Bailey was with Logan, which made sense now that everybody knew he had been at the top of the class in our year.

"Morgenstern, I choose you!" Dorian pointed at me, then the bench in front closest to the door.

"Peep?" Ember perched on the edge of the lab bench, blinking at us.

"Caw!" Mercy dive-bombed Ember, knocking her off the table. The critters soared up to tussle overhead. I knew it was playful since I could sense Ember's mood and Dorian smiled at their antics.

"Get your familiars under control and into the designated area, please."

As if in response to the professor, Seth barked at the pair of airborne playmates three times in rapid succession. Ember broke free, circling Mercy once before swooping down to rest on top of the little carpet-covered doghouse Seth hung out in during lab.

Mercy took a spin around the garbage can, which was empty, to her dismay. After that, she followed Ember, settling on the perch above her. It was almost like a pecking order, except the critter with the most authority was on the ground floor.

"Before we begin, I've got an announcement from Nurse Smith." The professor held a slip of paper up, reading from it. "Due to a delayed shipment of supplies, Familiar Bonding will begin tomorrow. Apologies for the late start."

"Saved by the USPS?" Dorian nudged me, winking.

"Ears open, mouths closed. This year's labs will expand on the themes we learned last year." Professor Luciano leaned his hands on the teacher's bench at the front of the room. A moment later, the cubbies under our benches opened, revealing the vintage 1980s trapper keepers that held our lab manuals. I ended up with the same unicorn as last year. Dorian's had a yin and yang symbol on it.

"Don't worry, class, we're starting with the basics this year. Safety!"

"Thank goodness," Logan muttered under his breath behind me.

"It's not all boring regulations and tours around the room." Professor Luciano grinned. "I'm also handing out a list of projects for the extramural lab collaboration exercises. Constructing these devices will require you to team up with students from the other two schools. If you try to do any of them with just magi, you will fail spectacularly."

"Is he always this gung-ho in here?" Dorian blinked. "I mean, in lecture, he's kinda blah."

"He loves the lab." I giggled behind my hand. "Maybe a little too much."

The tour was uneventful, as was the demonstration Professor Luciano did with all the safety equipment. It was a good thing, though. Either there had been additions to the equipment closets, or I'd forgotten some of what I learned last year. Maybe a little of both.

The list of collaborative projects was ten pages long. Each had a one-paragraph description, along with the recommended group makeup by extrahuman type. One was for making communication orbs, like the one I had smuggled onto the campus last year to communicate with Izzy and Cadence. This one could record and had a scrying feature. I tapped it with my finger, searching for my pencil with the other hand to circle it.

"Found your project?"

"Maybe. Depends. It says here we don't get teams assignments until October after the other schools send their groups over."

"You'll work with your friends from town, right?"

"Maybe, but a faculty member has to approve and supervise each group, and I like meeting new people." I blinked then put my hand over my mouth.

"Self-discovery is a pretty amazing thing," Dorian said that like he'd been around that block a time or five.

"Totally."

As it turned out, I discovered more than that in the month between the first day of lab and the beginning of extramurals. Not all of it was so hopeful, either.

CHAPTER SIXTEEN

The breakfast crowd could be intimidating, but at dinner, most of us sat in the lounge with takeout bags. Since Grace and Dorian stuck to the cafeteria that day, I was out there with Dylan and Eston, who wasn't a huge fan of crowds. Dylan wanted to avoid Grace, and I liked going over the day's notes in relative quiet.

Arick Magnuson approached me then and stood, shifting his weight from one foot to the other.

"Hi, Arick Magnuson." I grinned. "Have a seat."

"Thanks?" He sat on the edge of an ottoman none of us was using. "So, I heard a number of things about you yesterday, and I have a question."

"Yeah, she's really an extramagus. No, she's not evil. And unfortunately for her, she's Alex Onassis's ex-girlfriend. Did I cover everything?" Dylan's nostrils flared. "Enough to take back to Tempe?"

"No." Arick blinked, then turned away from Dylan to look at me. "You found a dragonet to bond with, and Elanor Pierce said you helped her brother and his roommate find their familiars. Since I don't have one, I was hoping— "

Arick hung his head to hide his reddening face, which was a lost cause. I tried to remember being this out of sorts. It felt like ages since then. Maybe I didn't need a point of reference. Bubbe said empathy could work without that. It seemed like a good time to try.

"As far as Ember goes, she found me. I didn't go looking, and anyway, there's no wrong or right way to meet the right critter. Familiar Bonding will help. I'm taking it as an elective, so I'll see you there."

"Really?"

Eston's big black dog circled Arick. The canine was dour and fiercely protective of his magus. The new kid froze in place. Once his critter finished his appraisal, Eston looked up, catching Arick's gaze and staring into his eyes. After a moment, he spoke.

"Nobody in your family does familiar magic, so why are you at Hawthorn Academy?" Eston tilted his head, adjusting his glasses. He didn't blink.

"I've been reading about them my whole life. They're the only thing I ever wanted to study. Nothing else back home in Bergen felt right to me."

"That'll do." Eston nodded, then gazed at my page of lecture notes. He was with Dylan in Professor DeBeers' class, and part of what we did over lounge dinners was look over each other's coursework.

"I still don't know about this kid." Dylan crossed his arms over his chest. Even Gale peeked out from behind his head to give Arick a withering glare. "If he's carrying tales, I'll find out."

"Go easy." I shook my head. "He's a first-year, and not even from this country. Like you, Dylan."

"And Alex last year. I think caution's wise." Unfortunately, Dylan made sense.

"I'm giving him a chance. If you guys don't want to, that's your decision." I shrugged. "Don't try to stop me from helping."

Dylan dropped his arms, and Gale eased his stance.

"Thanks." Arick exhaled. "You don't know how much of a relief it is to hear that."

"You should get some food before they close the caf." I jerked my chin at the doorway.

"Yeah. Right." Arick looked everywhere but at our faces. "Maybe tomorrow, I can get takeout like you guys?"

"Hang on, this is my duty as a food services employee." Dylan tore a section of brown paper from his own bag and pulled a pen out of his pocket. He sketched a quick though sloppy map. "That's how you get to the takeaway window. Ask for Penelope."

Arick nodded, saying nothing else. He stood and tucked the makeshift map in his back pocket before hurrying away. I noticed a series of four small and jagged tears in the tail of his blazer. Had he been in a fight? If so, why hadn't he mentioned it?

"That might come back to bite you." Eston shook his head.

"He doesn't seem evil." I raised my eyebrow.

"It's not him. The damage on his blazer means Tempe's singled him out." Eston pointed at his dog's nose. "Grundylow claws."

"It's Grace's deal to navigate popularity oceans. She's like a captain." I shrugged. "We don't have to look popular."

"What's our job, then?" Eston tilted his head.

"We're the brute squad." I leaned back in my comfy chair. "I'm the scary extramagus. Don't make me lose my temper."

"Yeah. They won't like Aliyah when she's angry." Dylan smirked. "Good thing you're not always angry."

I laughed, relieved to hear him crack a joke. Last year he was the class clown, after all.

"That's fine and well." Eston nodded. "You're athletes, the closest thing we have to jocks. But I'm kind of not that."

"I'm the brawn, like John Luther." Dylan leaned forward, elbows on his knees. "But you're like Sherlock Holmes, making sense of everything."

"Ah. The brain." Eston nodded, adjusting his glasses.

"Bingo."

"Speaking of brains, we should go over this list of projects." I tapped the stapled packet of papers. "Work out a strategy."

"Shouldn't we have Logan's help with that?"

"Help with what now?" Logan leaned in the doorway.

"This list. We've got to narrow it down." I flipped to the second page. "This orb device looks like a challenge, but one we can handle for sure."

"Because of your friends in town?"

"That's right. I'm going to see Izzy and Cadence this weekend and talk to them about potential teammates from their schools."

"This project requires changelings." Eston adjusted his glasses.

"I know two, Azrael Ambersmith and Brianna Collins. They're both goblins."

"Good." Eston nodded. "Goblins are masters of illusion, perfect for a visual display. But we've only got one Umbral Magus in our year. That's Grace."

"What's a good stand-in?" Dylan flipped to the last page, a list of extrahuman subtypes. "Not solar, right?"

"Undeath." Logan nodded without even looking at the paper. "Faith can do it if Grace isn't on the orb team. And fire will help, so either Kitty or Aliyah."

"This is college-level magical theory stuff, Logan. Have you been studying all summer?" Eston blinked.

"Pretty much. Mrs. Morgenstern loaned me a couple of books."

"Wow." He grinned. "We should hang sometime and talk theory. I love this stuff, and my folks don't get it."

"I'd like that." Logan smiled.

Dylan got preoccupied all of a sudden with a patch of dry scales on Gale's neck. I couldn't blame him. The look on his face reminded me of how I'd felt last year when Noah focused on his school friends and left me behind. Back then, I'd needed a friend, so it was time to be one.

"The Magipsych Fair isn't all we've got to worry about." I elbowed him. "We should do some extra practice before Bishop's Row tryouts. Together."

"We're going to have company, though." Dylan gazed at his shoes. "I asked Lee to practice with me already and he said yes."

"That's cool."

It's not, and you know it. You wanted time alone with Dylan. Tell him it's not okay.

"Hey, are you going to eat that?" Dylan pointed at my side of coleslaw.

"Down the bottomless pit it goes, I guess." I handed it to him, glad to see his appetite coming back.

The Evil Inside Voice was right. I wasn't happy about sharing my time with Dylan, but it couldn't be helped. Maybe it was better for him to have more friends around than just me anyway.

Dylan Khan was not okay, no matter what he said. Maybe branching out would help him get better.

I did a full sweep of the third-floor bathroom despite being tired. Eight was the hour I usually started winding down before bed at Hawthorn Academy, not ideal for swimming, but Faith wanted to meet, and I'd agreed. I had to make sure none of the first-years lurked in a stall or the changing rooms first.

The bathrooms at Hawthorn Academy were enormous, outfitted with the usual sinks, toilets, and showers. They had a couple of old-fashioned clawfoot tubs as well, but the main feature was the Roman Bath, which was like a swimming pool, deep and long enough to swim laps in.

The campus between worlds had unlimited space when it was built, and everything classical in an ancient sense had been in style back then. While attendance had been low since the Reveal, the Hawkins family hadn't decreased the campus's size from the old days.

Faith Fairbanks took full advantage of that. Swimming was her preferred sport. Growing up in Salem meant I'd become adept at it too. It wasn't my favorite physical activity, but I could keep up with her.

I'd gone into a stall to put on my bathing suit. When I emerged, Faith was already at the side of the bath. Ember swooped down from her perch, landing beside Seth. He pranced and capered, letting out a series of short happy barks in response to her peeps. It was nice to see them relax and play together.

Faith sat at the edge of the pool, her legs in the water. I joined her.

"So, what's this about Alex?" I stuck my tongue out and blew a raspberry. "Sorry. Thinking about him brings out my inner sixth-grader."

"No need to apologize. He sucks." Faith snorted. "But I think I can keep him from being too much trouble."

"What's the idea?"

"For you, distraction. My plan is to zap him from time to time with a little undeath energy. He'll get sluggish. Since he always plays up that cold-blooded snake vibe, acting like he's not a threat, no one should notice, but just in case—"

"You need me to light things up?" I shook my head, chuckling. "Fire didn't work out so well for me last year."

"You've got way more control now, Aliyah." Faith kicked a foot, splashing. "Anyway, you can choose which shiny magic to use. Solar's less flammable, right?"

"Yeah, it's safer." I grinned.

"Bonus points if they think it was Noah." Faith turned her head, looking me in the eye. "Everybody knows he still hates Alex because of the whole Darren thing last year."

"I didn't even think of that." I sighed. "Some schemer I am, huh?"

"You are definitely not evil overlord material, but I've got it covered."

"Because you're evil?" I blinked. "You, the doting girlfriend?"

"I had the upbringing for it, which doesn't miraculously vanish just because I decided to reject it." She looked up, eyes as limpid as the pool, and colder. "I'm using everything I learned at home for good now."

"Heaven help Hal's Mom, then." I eased off the topic of Faith's family.

"You don't know the half of it. She is going to be in deep shit once it hits the fan."

"I thought the custody hearing happened already?"

"There's one more in May. Anyway, the last one opened a can of worms, for Mrs. Hawkins, anyway." Faith sighed. "I'm all for escaping your toxic family, but once you hurt the family you choose, all bets are off."

"What do you mean?" I raised an eyebrow.

"She married, had a kid. That's her family now, and she screwed them over. That hearing only hinted that she's a dhampyr, but her family will find her sooner or later." She crossed her arms, rubbing them with her hands. "They're probably horrible people."

"Are you sure?"

"No, but it's logical." She closed her eyes. "Now we have to worry about them showing up out of the blue."

"If she'd been honest with the doctors, medical privacy would have protected her and Hal. There wouldn't have been any stories in the paper."

"Karma isn't real, but coincidence is, and even more of a bitch."

"They're Hal's family too." I reached out, patted her shoulder. "Maybe he takes after them, and there's nothing to be afraid of."

"I'm not scared of vampires. I told Hal to let them come and catch these hands." She held them up, palms out toward the water, staring at the backs of them.

Usually, Faith would grin or snort to indicate sarcasm, but her statement carried no humor. This was deadly serious to her. She'd risk death to protect Hal. It reminded me of how devoted my parents were to each other.

"Neither am I. Fire hands, remember? But nothing says they have to be monstrous."

"Stephanie's age makes it likelier. Her parents had her before the Reveal, and with pre-reveal vamps, you never know. That isn't just shitty Fairbanks family philosophy, either. Remember the turning spree that generation did back in the day?"

"I do. I'm a Night Creatures fan." I sighed. "And I'm half-Hopewell. Nothing like finding out your uncle tried to take over two worlds to give you a perspective on twisted family trees. I'll keep hoping they're outliers and decent folk. I mean, Hal's one of the best people we know, right?"

"I'd hope right along with you, but Mrs. Hawkins is way too fearful. I watched her face throughout the hearing."

"Sometimes, I think you've seen way more than anyone our age should have."

"Whatever." She pushed off from the edge of the pool into the water. "Enough gloom and doom. Let's swim."

We spent the next hour doing exactly that. The water couldn't wash away the sins of our families, but it helped us forget them for a little while.

CHAPTER SEVENTEEN

Familiar Bonding was in the infirmary, which was the closest thing Hawthorn Academy had to a basement. Along with the ramp leading down from the main floor, the infirmary also had no windows. This was good because one of the infirmary staff, my favorite, was a vampire.

Ezekiel Brown greeted me with a grin and a slight nod. I hadn't seen him since last year, so I smiled back.

"Hi, Zeke!"

"Miss Morgenstern, what brings you here at this time of day?"

"Familiar Bonding."

"You hardly need it this year."

"I kind of think it's fun." I indicated Ember, who let out a loud snore from my shoulder. "Anyway, Logan's bringing Dorian Spanos because he's new to familiars. He's got an unruly gryphon. Maybe I can help."

"Those are sound reasons." Ezekiel nodded. "Although I had assumed you dropped by to visit with young Master Hawkins and Miss Fairbanks."

"Oh, they're here?" I clapped, waking Ember.

"Yes. Just a moment, and I'll see how amenable they are to a brief visit."

"Thanks, Zeke."

While waiting, I paced the room. This area of the infirmary included Nurse Smith's varnished pine desk, a line of chairs, and Ezekiel's antique roll-top writing desk, which stood beside the first aid cabinet. Ember fluttered to her favorite perch from last year atop the cabinet, but she'd grown and didn't fit anymore. The formerly cozy nook was now a tight and unpleasant squeeze.

"Peep." Ember flew back down to my shoulder, tucking herself around the back of my neck and slumping down. I sensed her disappointment

"It's okay, girl. Everybody grows." I shrugged. "Kind of a fact of life."

"You take the good, you take the bad." Dorian Spanos sauntered through the door. Mercy swooped in behind him, soaring in a figure-eight overhead.

"What?" I blinked.

"I guess I'm the only one at Hawthorn obsessed with eighties sitcoms." He sighed as Mercy took off from his shoulder to fly around the room. "At least tell me you've seen the *Golden Girls*."

"Only because of Noah." I shrugged. "Though that was a few years back."

"I think he needs to re-watch it." Dorian shook his head. "Your brother isn't the kind of person I'd thank for being a friend."

"Is he giving you crap?" I put my hands on my hips. "If so, I'll have words with him. Totally not cool to grief the new kid."

"Nope. Just plain old snobbery." Dorian shrugged.

"Yep, sounds like my brother."

"Crap on a crap cracker." Dorian stared at the ceiling, blinking and stepping backward. "Look out below!"

I craned my neck up, just barely making out the winged shape above the chandelier's orbs of light. It was Mercy, of course, and she had something lumpy and rank-smelling that rustled in her talons. Doris, who'd just walked through the door, looked up at the gryphon and hissed.

I didn't run, dodge, or duck and cover. Maybe I should have. Dorian's familiar wasn't up there for her health. Oh, no, nothing as simple as a playful romp or one-sided game of tag for Mercy the trash gryphon. I heard a tearing sound. Doris turned tail and fled, caterwauling down the hall.

She's been in the waste bin. That's the trash bag.

"Eww, gross!" I tried to fend off the garbage raining down on my head. Fortunately, Mercy hadn't explored the biohazard container or the one with sharps, but I did not appreciate having a musty banana peel for a hair accessory.

"Peep!" Ember untangled herself from my shoulders and leaped into the air, snagging the fruity refuse off my head. She deposited it in the nearest trash receptacle, which didn't have a bag anymore. The remnants of that hung from Mercy's talons in long plastic shreds.

The entire floor of the infirmary's front room was a minefield of refuse. I glanced at the side of the trash can and noticed the extra bag hanging over its side. After stepping over a few pieces of debris, I snatched it and began collecting bits and bobs from the floor. Dorian rushed to help, but he didn't look where he was going and ended up slipping in something orange.

"Whoa!" He managed to keep his balance, a good thing because if he'd fallen, he would've ended up with a partially full container of yogurt on his backside.

"What's going on in here?" Nurse Smith tapped his foot in the doorway.

"Just reporting for Familiar Bonding. I guess we need it." I glanced up, dropping a handful of odorous crumb-coated plastic wrap into the trash bag.

"There's no way Ember's responsible for this mess." Nurse Smith put his hands on his hips, glaring at Dorian. "Hup!"

Dorian's demeanor changed like lightning, and he stood at attention. He looked like someone auditioning for a role in *A Few Good Men*, a far cry from his smirking nonchalance in class and whiny defiance at Gym.

"It's Mercy's fault, Sir."

"Caw!" Mercy swooped down, dive-bombing Nurse Smith's desk. She landed beside the placard with his name on it, peering at the shiny surface with curiosity blazing in her eyes.

"Don't you dare." Dorian snapped at his familiar, hands still and straight at his sides. "This is our last chance." He looked right through me, his lower lip trembling.

Somebody wasn't supposed to spill those particular beans.

"I care about the health and safety of everyone on this campus." Nurse Smith dropped his arms. "Working with a familiar takes practice, and you're a year behind. Bonus points for bonding with a gryphon. They're a handful but not the worst. That honor belongs to the karkinos." He patted the pocket on his scrub top. "That's why I run Familiar Bonding. Take it one day at a time. Messes can be cleaned up, and most faculty and staff here accept apologies. Unlike the school you came from."

"Thank you, sir." Dorian cleared his throat. "Did you go to the Academy?"

"Let's just say I'm in the know." Nurse Smith shook his head. "If you have trouble with your gryphon again, come straight to me. Understand, Spanos?"

"Yes, Nurse Smith."

"Good. Now help clean this up. We've got first-years without familiars on their way."

Dorian nodded, then moved to help me. After we finished getting the trash laden bag into the can, we moved to the sink in the corner and washed our hands.

"Your hair still has banana in it." He reached up and plucked a string from the peel off my head, washing it down the sink. "Sorry about that."

"The day I met Ember, she got stuck in my updo, so I've had worse critter-related insults to my hair. I'm fine."

He nodded, opening his mouth. Before Dorian could speak, Ezekiel emerged from the treatment room. He shook his head, placing one finger over his lips.

"They've fallen asleep. Since there's time before the dinner hour, I'll let them rest."

"Good choice." Nurse Smith nodded. "Please get the other room ready. I'm off to fetch the guest critters."

As the infirmary staff went about their business, Dorian and I found seats. Mercy perched on his arm and he shook his head at her, reaching down to stroke the feathers under her chin.

"What's gotten into you, girl?" He sighed. "Not enough open sky?"

"Gryphons are pretty adaptable, Dorian. There's enough room for airborne critters to stretch their wings here. Maybe she's not used to so many other animals around. You said you found her alone, right?"

"It was weird." Dorian shook his head. "Random. Not anything that's ever happened at the Academy before. The campus has wards to keep magical animals out, so—"

Logan interrupted by stepping through the doorway.

"Hey, are you okay?" He put his hand on Dorian's shoulder. "Doris told me about the trash."

"I'm still a little meh." Dorian gazed up at Logan, who blushed and looked away, dropping his hand. "But I will be okay in a few minutes."

"Am I interrupting something?"

I looked up to see Arick Magnuson standing in the doorway. His hair was wet enough to drip and he was missing his blazer, which reminded me of my misadventures last year.

"No, but what about you?" I gestured at him. "You look, um, rumpled."

"I'm okay now, I guess. It's been a rough day." He looked at his shoes. "Nothing like what the other kids in my year say about yours, though. No fires."

"One of those was my fault." Logan shook his head. "Lab accident. But yeah, we had an incendiary start last year."

"Where did you hear that, anyway?" Dorian crossed his arms over his chest. "Alex Onassis, by any chance?"

"No way." Arick shook his head. "He barely talks to anyone unless Temperance tells him to."

"You only answered one of my questions, kid." Dorian gave Arick so much side-eye he could have been a fish.

"Don't be so hard on him, Dorian." I shook my head. "We don't need to know the rumor mill's exact details."

"Just trying to cover all the angles." Dorian shrugged. "Don't want to assume."

"Someone's got to be a skeptic, I guess," said Logan.

"I'm not trying to tell you the earth is flat or anything." Arick blinked. "Anyway, I'm sorry. Repeating rumors isn't nice, and you guys are stuck with me for a month. Sorry."

The looks we shot at each other after Arick's self-deprecating statement could have come from the OK Corral. Maybe I relied on too much hyperbole, but the agitation level was supercharged. They barely noticed when the other first-year with no familiar, Michelina Zanelli, took the seat nearest to the door. She sat with her head down over folded hands. I couldn't see her face from behind the thick sheet of hair.

It all defused when Nurse Smith returned, pushing the cart with the unbound critters, just as he had last year. We stood up and followed him as he wheeled it into the larger treatment room.

He didn't give any explanations. Logan handed around his battered notebook from last year, which they flipped through avidly. As for me, everything from Familiar Bonding was second nature after growing up in a house over an extraveterinary office.

When Nurse Smith let the critters out, they ambled around, checking each of us out. I held my hand down for each of them in turn, setting an example of how to behave around unfamiliar animals.

Logan followed suit because he had at least as much experience with meeting new critters as I did. Despite our drastically different sources, some knowledge was common between showbiz and medicine. Dorian left the notebook to the others and kept trying unsuccessfully to coax Mercy down from the chandelier.

Last year, Dylan and Logan had been reluctant to interact with the unbonded animals at Familiar Bonding. Arick was totally the opposite. If anything, he was too eager. Even the friendly poodle seemed wary of his attention. Michelina sat still and let them come to her.

Eventually, a possum with golden fur and a yellow tail climbed into her lap, though she only patted its back a few times hesitantly.

I tried to keep my observation of the quiet girl covert, but that didn't work so well. The main thing I noticed about Michelina Zanelli was how careful she was, like she thought the whole world watched her. I realized Elanor Pierce had this same trait, but the difference was, Elanor loved an audience. Michelina dreaded it.

"Hi, I'm Aliyah," I said after moving to the seat beside her.

"Lena." She didn't look up.

"The possum likes you, Lena."

"Okay." Her voice cracked, and she covered her face with her hands.

I didn't know what to think about that, let alone do. I looked up, hoping for help from my fellow students, but Logan was busy explaining something to Arick while Dorian played tug-of-war with Mercy, who'd finally alighted on the floor. Fortunately, they were using a pull toy from the box in the corner instead of medical supplies.

"Hmm. Class is over for now, though I've got a few words for you all." Nurse Smith looked up from the notes on his clipboard. "This year, we'll do a selection of worksheets. At the very least, it will reinforce some of your lessons from the lectures."

"Are you saying we won't get to play with the animals tomorrow?" Arick stared at Nurse Smith like a disappointed puppy.

"I'm saying both you and Mr. Spanos need more information than you have about magical animals. Most of the families who send their children here have familiars in the house. With Mr. Spanos, most of his relatives are psychic and unable to bond with a familiar. But you, Mr. Magnuson?" Nurse Smith tapped his pen on the paper. "You're an enigma."

"Sorry." He winced. "My dad said something like that last week."

"Nothing to apologize for, as long as you're willing to do the work."

"I understand." He nodded. "And I am."

"What about Lena?" I asked, determined to speak up for the shy girl. Nurse Smith didn't get to answer.

The story continues with book Five, *Light of Equality*, coming soon to Amazon and Kindle Unlimited.

GLOSSARY

People

- **Changeling**- A mortal child of either one or two faerie parents. Most changelings choose a monarch sometime in their twenties, although some do it earlier than they have to.
- **Dampyr**- The mortal offspring of two vampires. They aren't as rare as many suspect, although because their blood is exceptionally sustaining to vampires, they keep their status secret. Dampyr sometimes have magic or psychic powers that work unreliably.
- **Faerie**- A term used to describe either a changeling who has tithed to a monarch and spent a year and a day in the Under or the pure creatures such as Gnomes and Pixies who were created by the king and queen.
- **Ghost**- A dead person with unfinished business becomes a ghost. If a mortal makes a contract before death, that gives them unfinished business and lets them linger. When ghosts finish their business, they move on, but no one knows where they go from here.
- **Magus**- A mortal who can use magic. Magic comes from

energy in the world. Most magi can only use one type of magic. However, a rare few can do more than one kind. Those are called extramagi.

- **Merfolk**- People who can live on land with legs or in the sea with fins and tails. They only emerged from the ocean after the Big Reveal and are still extremely rare outside of harbor towns.
- **Psychic**- A mortal with psychic power. Psychic ability comes from a person's own body and mind.
- **Vampire**- An unliving person who drinks blood to survive and enhance their abilities. Only regular mortals, psychics, and magi can get turned into vampires. Shifters, changelings, and faeries won't turn, and most of those won't survive an attempt.
- **Shifter**- A mortal who can take an animal's shape. Shifters have one form, with coloring similar to what they have while human. They usually have an enhanced sense while human-shaped, which goes along with their animal. For example, an owl shifter might have keen eyesight and a wolf shifter, a great sense of smell.

Shifter Varieties

- **Dragon**- The only shifters who can see both magic and psychic abilities, though only while shifted. The most powerful ones can partially shapeshift. Dragons are immortal and reproduce infrequently. There are so few of them since the Reveal that they've started taking other magical shifters as mates.
- **Kelpie**- A magical shifter who gets their abilities from an enchanted faerie pelt that bonds with their soul. The Kelpie pelts were created by the Goblin King, so they have Unseelie energy and restrictions. A Kelpie's animal form is a horse. Families pass the pelts down through generations,

and part of each ancestor lives on to help their descendants. The ancestors can get distracting, however.

- **Selkie**- A magical shifter who gets their abilities from an enchanted faerie pelt that bonds with their soul. The Selkie pelts were created by the Sidhe queen, so they have Seelie energy and restrictions. A Selkie's animal form is a seal or sometimes a sea otter. They can use water magic as long as they wear the pelt. Families pass the pelts down through the generations, and part of each ancestor lives on to help their descendants. The ancestors can get distracting, however.
- **Tanuki**- A magical shifter with enhanced speed and the ability to see all types of magic while shifted. They are also the only creatures who can manipulate luck, causing it to turn from good to bad or the other way around. They stop aging if they own a charm infused with luck from humans. Very few of those charms exist, having been either used up during the Reveal or locked away.

Powers

- **Air magic**- The power to conjure, control, and banish wind or air.
- **Earth magic**- The power to conjure, control, and banish earth, sand, or rock.
- **Empathy**- A psychic power to sense and influence emotions in other people.
- **Fire magic**- The power to conjure, control, and banish flames.
- **Ice magic**- The power to conjure, control, and banish ice.
- **Lightning magic**- The power to conjure, control, and banish lightning.
- **Poison magic**- The power to conjure, control, and banish poison. Each magus has a slightly different type of toxin they produce. Some are even antidotes to others.
- **Precognitive**- A psychic power to foretell future events.

- **Spectral magic**- the power to conjure, control, and banish light.
- **Spectral Affinity**- A trait some spectral magi have that makes them charismatic and believable.
- **Summoner**- A psychic power that lets the user make contracts with pure faeries, letting the summoner call them in times of need. Each creature has an anchor, some item symbolizing the bond. Mastery of summoning takes decades of study, which is why the most powerful are either vampires or past middle age.
- **Seelie**- The Sidhe queen's court. The Seelie way is about following the letter of the law, even when it's hard or cruel. They have a hard time reconciling faerie rules with the new mortal laws since the Big Reveal.
- **Solar Magic**- The power to conjure, control, or banish sunlight. Some of the most powerful practitioners can find hidden objects or discover long-kept secrets.
- **Solar Affinity**- A trait some solar magi have that makes them beacons for coincidence.
- **Space magic**- The power to move the self or objects instantly across distances. Some can even move other people.
- **Space Affinity**- This space power comes with an ability to locate people or things important to the magus.
- **Telekinesis**- A psychic power that moves objects.
- **Telepathy**- A psychic power to read minds.
- **Tithe**- The process of pledging to either the queen or king, making a changeling choose to be either Seelie or Unseelie.
- **Umbral magic**- The power to conjure, control, and banish shadows and veil or camouflage objects or people.
- **Umbral Affinity**- A trait some umbral magi have that makes them difficult to remember without psychic ability, faerie magic, or a shifter pack bond.
- **Undeath magic**- The power to conjure, control, and banish unliving energy.

- **Unseelie**- The Goblin king's court. The Unseelies bend the rules and often navigate mortal society more easily than their Seelie counterparts.
- **Water magic**- The power to conjure, banish, and control water.
- **Wood magic**- The power to conjure, banish, and control wood. It takes extreme power to influencing a living plant.

Creatures

- **Basilisk**- A venomous serpent that also has poison magic.
- **Dragonet**- A tiny dragon-like creature, always associated with one or more element which powers their breath attacks later in life. They have scales but are warm-blooded like birds. Most don't get much bigger than a small cat.
- **Familiar**- A magical or mythical creature who makes a bond with a magus.
- **Gryphon**- A chimera which has the head of a bird and hindquarters of a predatory mammal. They come in several combinations of base species, and habitat influences their choice in magi to bond with.
- **Karkus**- A crab that can change its shape. They're said to be the offspring of the crab that pinched Hercules as he battled the Hydra.
- **Lightning Bird**- A familiar from South Africa with an affinity for lightning. Its beak can jump-start a car.
- **Mercat**- A shapeshifting feline with fur for land and scales in the water. They can live in lakes, rivers, or in the sea as well as on land. They must never completely dry out, or they will die.
- **Moon Hare**- A magical rabbit that gets power from its particular moon phase. They commonly bond with umbral magi.
- **Pharaoh's Rat**- These natural predators of dragon shifters are the size of ferrets and resemble a mongoose with more

fur. They have an affinity for space magic and can use it on occasion.

- **Pigeon**- Not as mundane as most think, some pigeons have an uncanny sense of direction due to their affinity for air magic.
- **Pricus**- An aquatic goat said to be descended from Capricorn. They can warp time even better than Gnomes.
- **Pure Faeries**- Creatures who spring to life from magical sources in the Under. They are genderless, and their type and ability depend on place of origin. They're associated with only one court, although they will work together to defeat a common enemy.
- **Sand Cat**- A feline that lives in the desert, able to go for weeks without water. Earth magic lets them do this.
- **Sha**- A magical desert dog from Egypt. Sha are the size of mundane toy breeds with short hair and small pointy ears. They could pass for mundane except for their blue tongues. They are attracted to anything undead.
- **Sphinx**- A magic cat with an affinity for fire. The reason they're hairless is that they're resistant to flames.
- **Strix**- A venomous owl with an affinity for poison. Female striges have rounded tufts on their heads, while males have pointed ones.
- **Sumxu**- A lop-eared cat found only in northern China. They are masters of camouflage and have an affinity for several kinds of magic.

Places

- **The Academy**—Something between a community college and a military academy for extrahumans, the Academy is geared toward helping extrahumans who don't play well with mortals get ready to join a blended society. It's got divisions for learners of all ages, though they are housed separately.

- **Cherry Blossom School**- A dojo geared toward teaching extrahumans self-restraint, meditation, and how to temper their enhanced physical abilities with more mundane skills. It's been around for close to a hundred years, run by the Ichiro family. Mundane classes used to be offered as a front but now are a separate division.
- **Ellicot City Magitechnic**- A prep school for magi and psychics specializing in magipsychic technology. It's located outside Baltimore.
- **Gallows Hill School**- Traditionally for shifters, this prep school in Salem recently opened its doors to changelings and other extrahumans not categorized as magi or psychics.
- **Hawthorn Academy**- A preparatory school for magi in Salem. Its campus is in the space between the mortal realm and the Under, giving it unrivaled privacy. They specialize in teaching familiar magic.
- **Providence Paranormal College**- A school founded just one year after Brown University and located right in its shadow. Providence Paranormal used to admit only magi and psychics, but it's been accepting all types of extrahumans ever since Henrietta Thurston became headmistress. There has been trouble since then for students and faculty, leading people to believe dissenters are sabotaging the school.
- **Trout Academy**- A prestigious preparatory school for changelings with magic, recently open to magi and magical shifters. Its campus is located in South County and has been operating in some form or another since Rhode Island Colony was founded.
- **The Under**- The faerie realm. It's been divided into two parts ever since the Sidhe Queen and the Goblin king split up thousands of years ago. Mortals don't age in the Under, but it's a dangerous place for them to be. Getting lost means never being seen again, and it's easy to get indebted to

something nasty while trying to get through or out of the Under.

- **Wolf Messing Prep**- An institute for psychics to learn to control their skills before heading to college.

Events

- **The Big Reveal**- The term used for the 1990s, when the world discovered magic was real and extrahumans existed. The decade was marked with fear as everyone adjusted to the changes. Since the 21st Century, law and technology work for both humans and extrahumans.
- **Boston Internment**- A reaction by Boston government officials to the disappearance and suspected trafficking in extrahumans, especially shifters. All registered extrahumans in Boston lived on barges for close to a month under guard by the Boston Police. The traffickers got their hands on some magical gadgets, rendering the protection useless. Few survived.

THANK YOU!

Thank you for reading! If you loved this book, please leave a review. You can find my other work by clicking the links below, going to **my website** or visiting my **Author Central page**.

ALSO BY D.R. PERRY

Providence Paranormal College

Bearly Awake (Book 1)

Fangs for the Memories (Book 2)

Of Wolf and Peace (Book 3)

Dragon My Heart Around (Book 4)

Djinn and Bear It (Book 5)

Roundtable Redcap (Book 6)

Better Off Undead (Book 7)

Ghost of a Chance (Book 8)

Nine Lives (Book 9)

Fan or Fan Knot (Book 10)

Hawthorn Academy

Familiar Strangers (Book 1)

Acting in Kindness (Book 2)

Fire of Justice (Book 3)

Learning to Give (Book 4)

Gallows Hill Academy

Year One: Sorrow and Joy (Book one)

For other books by DR Perry please see her Amazon author page.

CONNECT WITH THE AUTHOR

Website: https://www.drperryauthor.com/

Join her newsletter!

Find more of D.R. Perry's books on Amazon.

OTHER LMBPN PUBLISHING BOOKS

To be notified of new releases and special promotions from LMBPN publishing, please join our email list:

http://lmbpn.com/email/

For a complete list of books published by LMBPN please visit the following pages:

https://lmbpn.com/books-by-lmbpn-publishing/